A VAGUELY MUFFLED ~~ ~~ ~~INTERING GLASS issued from ab~~ ~~. Whatever it was, it had smashed a window.

Not an animal.

The rush of fear hit Devin hard and fast. It was stronger even than it had been when the car had cut him off in the road. This felt as if something in his chest had grabbed his heart and was trying to force it out of his mouth.

Human?

"This isn't over."

Could it be the Slits? Had they followed him?

Above and deeper inside the house, it sounded like the furniture was being pushed around in the master bedroom suite.

"It's inside," Karston squealed, his thin voice whiny and afraid.

WICKED DEAD
DEAD
TORN

BY

STEFAN PETRUCHA
AND THOMAS PENDLETON

HarperTeen

AN IMPRINT OF HarperCollinsPublishers

Grateful acknowledgment is given to Shaun O'Boyle
for the use of the title page image, © Shaun O'Boyle. More
of his evocative photographs can be seen on
www.oboylephoto.com.

HarperTeen is an imprint of
HarperCollins Publishers.

Library of Congress Cataloging-in-Publication Data
Petrucha, Stefan.
    Torn / by Stefan Petrucha and Thomas Pendleton. — 1st
HarperTeen paperback ed.
        p.   cm. — (Wicked dead ; #2)
    Summary: Just when sixteen-year-old Devin's rock band,
Torn, is on the verge of success, its members are stalked by
a beast who is a ruthless killer.
    ISBN 978-0-06-113850-8 (pbk.)
    [1. Rock music—Fiction. 2. Bands (Music)—Fiction.
3. Monsters—Fiction. 4. Horror stories.] I. Pendleton,
Thomas, date. II. Title.
PZ7.P44727To 2007   2007012486
[Fic]—dc22   CIP
                                                            AC

Typography by Christopher Stengel

First Edition

THOMAS PENDLETON dedicates this book to JCP and all the wicked ones the world over.

STEFAN PETRUCHA dedicates this book to the dead—Martin, Felicia, Amelia, Michael, Frank, Mary, Joseph L., and the many others he does not know. He hopes you've all got a great game going somewhere.

PROLOGUE

A storm raged over Lockwood Orphanage. Wind
pounded through the eaves and played against the
rhythm of marching rain. Lightning flashed in the
wounded sky, bringing foul milky light to the black
windows. All through the night grim weather had
battered the roof and the sides of the six-story
Georgian, but now the storm was moving inside.

"She's here."

Two girls stood in the great room of the
orphanage amid a junk shop of tattered furniture.
A third girl, lovely and delicate with golden hair
dropping in long ringlets to her shoulders, sat
demurely, her thin nightgown pooling around her
on the cracked wooden floorboards.

1

All three trembled as the shadowed air around them rolled and swirled. A cloud took shape before them, vague at first, but more defined with each passing moment. A face appeared in the raven mist. It had a narrow nose and thin, mean lips. The cloud rolled out violently, as if exploding, then was drawn back into itself. Suddenly, the mist was gone, leaving a tall form in its place.

A woman.

The Headmistress.

She wore a long gray skirt and a white blouse with billowy loose sleeves that pinched down into broad starched cuffs at her wrists. A black brooch secured the collar of the blouse, which was so tight to her throat it would have strangled another woman. A living woman.

She stood straight-backed with her hands knotted at her waist. Her pitiless eyes searched the room. With a rapid flash of the irises, she took in the tall girl in men's striped pajamas and the pretty girl in the lovely nightgown sitting on the floor. Finally, her attention came to rest on the black-haired girl wearing a black T-shirt.

"We weren't doing anything," Anne said too quickly, crossing her arms over the front of her T-shirt. Though defiant, her voice was laced with fear.

"Indeed," the Headmistress said. "And yet, you all know the rules. None of you are allowed down here after lights out. But here you are. *Down here*. Where you're not supposed to be. So, in fact, you were doing something. Something quite wrong."

From her place on the floor, Mary lowered her head. She plucked at the hem of her nightgown nervously, then smoothed it.

"We were looking for Shirley," Daphne said, feeling waves of cold air rushing over her. Standing near the Headmistress always felt like being in an icebox. "We were playing a game upstairs, and she got frightened. You know how sensitive she is. We just came down to find her. We were going right back up."

The Headmistress nodded her head slowly. She cast a glance at Anne, who looked furious, with her jaw set tight. To Mary, she said, "Is this true?"

"Yes, Headmistress," Mary said, able to look at the woman for only a second.

"Then why do you appear ever so comfortable, sitting on that floor?"

"I tripped when you arrived."

"Clumsy, clumsy girl," the Headmistress said.

"Yes, Headmistress."

"This is lame. I'm going back up," Anne said. She

uncrossed her arms and began walking toward the great staircase. "Shirley can worry about herself."

"I think you'll wait," the Headmistress said. "I'm not quite convinced of your story's veracity."

Anne stopped in her tracks. She spun around, facing the Headmistress.

"Well, let's find Shirley," Daphne said, a bit too brightly. "She'll tell you. It really was just a stupid game."

"Indeed," the Headmistress said. "Let's do ask your little friend."

With that, the Headmistress cocked her head to the side and opened her mouth wide. A plume of vapor rolled over her lips, and encircled her head like a dark halo. The ring expanded in misty waves. As the ripples met and continued past them, each girl heard the same thing.

Shirley. Come to the great room AT ONCE!

The command was deafening. On the floor, Mary covered her ears, but it did no good. This was not a voice of lung and throat and tongue, but one of spirit. It rattled the very material of her being and spread through the orphanage in waves.

Daphne gasped at the sound. She shook her head rapidly to free herself of it.

"God!" Anne said. "Ever hear of a volume knob?"

"Silence," the Headmistress ordered.

"Great idea," Anne replied. "It's free, and it's for everyone. Try some."

"Anne," both Daphne and Mary said in warning.

"How dare you!" the Headmistress roared, reaching out to grasp Anne by the arm. "Your petulant mouth will get you a night in the Red Room."

"She didn't mean it." Daphne rushed forward to defend Anne. She knew the terrors of the Red Room. So did Anne, but the black-haired girl must not be thinking straight.

Anne looked from Daphne to Mary, who remained sitting. She looked back at the Headmistress, her expression still sour. "Yeah, right. I didn't mean it. Talk all you want. That's your thing. Enjoy. Just let me go."

"I'm not done with you, yet."

"The hell you're not." Anne yanked her arm hard and managed to free herself. She stumbled back a step, and then turned to escape, but she wasn't nearly fast enough. The Headmistress shot forward and again grabbed hold of Anne's arm.

"You little beast!" the Headmistress hissed. "You will behave."

"Stop," Daphne begged. "Please stop. Anne's just worried about Shirley. Really, she is."

"Shirley," Anne spat in disgust. "I couldn't care less about that whiny freak." She turned to the Headmistress. "And I couldn't care less about *you*. I'm tired of taking orders from you. We're dead. Do you get that? We've done our time. You have no right to tell me what to do. None. So go play *Mommie Dearest* with someone else, and get out of my face."

"Anne, please," Daphne pleaded.

Mary continued to fuss with the hem of her dress, unable to look up at the fight. Her mind raced. She wanted to help Anne. She really wanted to, but she couldn't stand up.

If she did, it would have dire consequences for them all.

So she remained on the floor, pretending to be absorbed by her gown.

The Headmistress pulled Anne close with one hand, while pushing Daphne away with the other. "Upstairs," she said, her eyes burning into Anne's.

"Screw you!" Anne cried, returning the Headmistress's gaze with equal fury. "You're not my mother or my master."

"You have no mother, child," the Headmistress said. "That's why you were brought here. As for being your master . . ."

The Headmistress blew apart into a cloud of vapor. Thin tendrils whipped out from the shadowy accumulation and wrapped around Anne's arms, her chest and her face. The girl's eyes grew wide with terror as more and more of her body became entwined by the misty ropes.

"Don't!" Daphne shouted.

"Let me go, you bitch!" Anne screamed.

She kicked her legs and thrashed her arms, but her struggle was futile. The dark mist had her bound; then it gagged her mouth. Only her eyes moved, looking desperate in her capture.

"Oh, Anne," Daphne whispered, hopelessly.

Then the cloud moved away, taking Anne with it. Across the great room. To the stairs. Up and up, until the only disturbance came from the storm wailing above the orphanage.

The girls fell silent.

Shirley, wearing her pink flannel gown, descended from the ceiling, walking like a crab down the flaking walls. She paused for a moment, searching the great room for the Headmistress, but all she saw was Daphne by the sofa, one hand covering her eyes, and Mary sitting on the floor, playing with the edge of her nightgown.

"Where is she?" Shirley whispered, too frightened to leave her place on the wall.

"She has departed," Mary said. "Like the unforgiving tide, she has crashed to the shore, taken her due, and withdrawn."

"Where's Anne?"

Mary opened her mouth to answer, but Daphne spoke first. "She went back upstairs. Just for a while." She knew the truth would upset Shirley, probably make her disappear again.

But Shirley already knew the truth.

"She's being punished, isn't she?" Shirley said, scurrying two feet up the wall. "Oh no, we're all going to be punished, aren't we? We shouldn't have come down here. We shouldn't have. It's against the rules. Oh, why did I let you talk me into this?"

"Calm down, kid," Daphne said, fully aware that it was just such an outburst from Shirley that had called the Headmistress in the first place. "Losing your head isn't going to help Anne now. It isn't going to help anything."

"But what are we going to do?" Shirley wondered aloud.

"We're going to keep cool heads," Daphne replied. "Now, come join us."

"We're not supposed to be down here."

"Fine," Daphne said, exasperated and in no mood for another argument. "You go on back up, and we'll meet you in the classroom."

Shirley looked around the room, seeming unsure. Then she raced back up the wall, disappearing into the ceiling as she had before the Headmistress's arrival.

Daphne crossed to where Mary sat on the floor. She looked down, perturbed at her friend. Through the whole ordeal with the Headmistress, Mary had done nothing. She'd just sat there. Such cowardice wasn't like Mary, and Daphne was greatly disappointed with her.

"Do you mind telling me why you were acting like a bump on a log while the forest was burning down around us?"

"I had to," Mary said quietly. She shifted slightly on the floor, getting her legs under her. She stood, brushing at the back of her nightgown. When she stepped to the side, Daphne saw Mary's excuse for keeping still.

On the floor, in the place where Mary's nightgown had pooled, sat a vermillion bag, the *Clutch*, and five small bones, still splayed out from their game. The tiny skull resting at the center lay on its side, one eye socket looking upward. It reminded Daphne of a wink.

She lunged forward and wrapped her arms around Mary. "Quick thinking. I'm sorry I questioned you."

"The Headmistress just appeared so fast. I didn't know what to do. The bones were all over the place, and the Clutch, and there just wasn't time to pick it all up. So I covered them, like a hen protecting her chicks."

"You're wonderful," Daphne said with a relieved chuckle. "Let's gather up those chicks and go find ourselves a chicken."

They found Shirley in the second-floor classroom. She sat in a shadowy back corner, her hands clutching the desk before her.

The room was even more dismal and depressing than the dilapidated great room below. Down there was dust and rot and general disarray, but up here . . .

Twenty weathered desk chairs sat in the gloomy space, four across and five back. A large oak desk faced the chairs from the front of the

10

room. Against the wall on the left, a broad map hung from ancient pins. The window across the room was broken, webbed with cracks; a fist-sized hole was punched through it, low and to the right. Wind rushed through. Everything here was filthy, but it was not otherwise different from the way it had been, unlike downstairs where vandals had overturned and damaged the furniture. It was the basically untouched appearance that gave the room its particularly horrific quality.

Once, children sat at these desks. They dreamed in these seats, looking through the window at the great world from which they were delivered. Now, the arched-back chairs were empty and frosted with dust. Gray like granite. They reminded Daphne of tombstones, marking the passing of countless young lives.

And did I once occupy one of these desks? Daphne wondered. *Did I learn here? Did I dream? Why can't I remember? Why can't any of us remember?*

"There's our delicate child," Mary said, pointing to where Shirley sat at the back of the class.

"What happened to Anne?" Shirley whispered. "What did the Headmistress do to her?"

"The Red Room," Daphne said. There was no point in lying about it. Shirley would pitch a fit, but it couldn't be helped. None of them was more terrified of the Red Room than Shirley, even though she was the only one never to have spent time there.

"Oh," Shirley yelped, clutching herself in fear. "What are we going to do?"

"We're going to wait for Anne," Mary said. "She'll need us when she emerges from that horrible place."

"What if the Headmistress comes back?"

"You know she has to guard the door," Daphne said. "She can't leave until she's finished with Anne. We have a few hours."

Shirley clamped her thumbnail between her teeth and looked around the room, as if expecting a monster to break through the walls. She gnawed on the nail and clutched her chest with the other arm.

"Should we play?" Mary whispered sheepishly.

"You mean the bones?" asked Daphne. "It is the perfect time, with the Headmistress occupied."

A gust of wind blew through the broken window. The paper map clicked against the wall.

"We can't," Shirley said quickly. "Anne isn't here."

"True enough," Daphne agreed. "But she just

won the game. She's already told a story, and it's unlikely she'd get another chance so soon. It couldn't hurt anything to play once more."

"I don't think it's fair to her," Shirley said, her voice barely a whisper.

"Well, what would you like to do?" Mary asked. "Should we count raindrops or motes of dust?"

"Aren't there other games we could play? The stories we tell are just so awful. Why can't we play a game that isn't *so awful*?"

"You know this game has a purpose," Daphne said, "and a real reward should we truly win."

"But how do you know?" Shirley asked, her voice very near tears. Her sullen face lowered. She removed her thumb from her teeth and set her hands on the desk. "How do you know we won't be here forever?"

Daphne stepped forward and leaned down to put her arm over the seated girl's shoulders. "You saw what happened to Sylvia. She was with us for a very long time until the night she told that story—*her* story. Don't you remember what she said? 'It's me. My god, this story is about me.'"

Mary came forward to stand next to them. Thinking of Sylvia, she recalled bits of a poem by

13

Byron, a poem of beauty, of light and of music. Under less somber circumstances she might have quoted from it. Instead, she put her lips very near Shirley's ear and said softly, "Don't you remember how beautiful it was? Don't you remember how she smiled so, *so* brightly? And then, her body turned to specks of shining white light, and she was gone."

"But we don't know where she went," Shirley argued, sniffling.

"Perhaps," Mary whispered, "but we know she moved on. I have to believe heaven finally made a place for her."

"Anne will be angry with us," Shirley said.

"Anne is always angry with us," Daphne replied, giving Shirley's shoulders a tight squeeze, knowing she was about to agree to the game. "Next time, we'll let her roll first, and she can take three turns if she wants."

"Maybe we just shouldn't tell her," Shirley suggested.

"A capital idea," Daphne said with a laugh. "So, you're in?"

Shirley let a smile creep over her tear-stained face. "Why? Are you writing a book?"

The girls laughed. Quickly Daphne pulled away

and spun one of the desk chairs to face Shirley's. Mary turned and gently brought another chair forward until the three desks formed a blunt triangle. She set the Clutch on the desk before her and waited. The familiar excitement of playing the game flooded her.

"Shall I?" Mary asked, indicating the vermillion bag.

"Well, Anne opened it last," Daphne said, "so it is your turn."

"But we won't tell Anne," Shirley insisted.

"We won't say a word," Mary promised.

With trembling fingers, Mary touched the smooth fabric. She stroked the velvet material, let her fingertips pause on the hard lumps made by the bones. She parted its mouth and upturned the Clutch. Bones, coppery with age, spilled into her palm. She felt the smooth side of the skull and the sharp points of claws. They tingled, as if eager to be rolled.

With a gentle shake she let the bones fall on the desk, and knew instantly that she had not won.

"My turn," Daphne said. But she too failed to roll the winning combination.

And so it went, one turn after another. Mary. Daphne. Shirley. Then Mary again. Excitement and disappointment mixed in the girls as each turn produced no winner.

"Maybe we can't play with just three," Shirley said, dejected after her last failed roll. "Maybe it has to be all four of us."

"We've rolled a lot longer than this with no winner," Daphne said. "Let's keep at it. Mary?"

And again the bones were in her hand: at turns soft and smooth, jagged and rough. Mary studied the tiny symbols etched into the bones. She concentrated on the one symbol that meant the most: the symbol that must appear on three of the bones for her to succeed.

She rolled.

"You did it," Shirley gasped, as if it were a genuine miracle.

The room around her grew very quiet, and Mary held her breath, waiting for the story. No sound of rain or thunder touched her now. Something was coming.

A great whooshing, like a hurricane wind, filled her head. There were faces and voices and odd machines . . .

Then there was music.

The band's intro by club owner Allen Bates was short and sweet. The thirtysomething entrepreneur grabbed the mike at the center of the small stage, brought it to his lips, and screamed "Torn!" like it was four syllables long. Then he stepped back, slamming his hands together wildly, nodding for the crowd to do the same. As the applause rose, blue lights came up on the five figures on Tunnel Vision's stage. Showtime.

Devin slammed an easy E on his refurbished Fender. Cheryl ripped along the drum kit, her hair flailing back and forth across her face like a long blond whip. Ben doubled Devin on the keyboard, and even the bassist, Karston, came in almost on time for a change. The sound rode the cheering, revving the crowd.

As the tempo built, square-jawed Cody, his bedhead spiky hair bleached white, leaped into a spotlight with a spanking new Les Paul hanging from his neck. His insanely deep, raspy voice flooded the room:

> *Wind up*
> *Going down*
> *I won't be your dancing clown!*
>
> *Eat this*
> *In your face*
> *Or disappear without a trace!*

It was an easy number, Devin thought as he watched and played. He could sleepwalk through the changes.

> *Aching brain coming out my skull,*
> *Looking back at the hole in my eyes.*
> *Just don't know who I am today—*
> *The mirror breaks and I die.*

Cheryl, her strong but feminine arms flashing

from her sleeves as she confidently crashed out the beat, stopped swinging her head long enough to give Devin a wide, sexy smile. "Face" was his song, the one that got them the gig. He smiled back, almost missing his harmony on the chorus:

And where were you
When I bled about our love?
And who were you
When I crawled from underground?

The crowd wasn't huge for a Friday night, but it was big enough, and everyone seemed to be enjoying themselves. Feet stomped, hands clapped, hips twitched. Torn was going over. It was a big night for their little nu-metal garage band.

Get out
Lock the door
I can't take you anymore.

Devin felt like he should be thrilled, proud, or pleased, but he wasn't any of those things. Instead, he felt out of it, like he was watching everything from somewhere far away, judging. Why? What was wrong with him? He had what any seventeen-year-old guitarist craved: a rock group finally breaking into the Macy club scene and a relationship with the hot drummer, but all he could manage was this weird disappointment, as if he'd gotten to the promised land, but it had turned out to be trashy.

It wasn't the club. The long, dark space with the curved fieldstone roof and walls used to be a train tunnel. What could be cooler than that? During the nineties freight trains used it to carry textiles in and out of the adjoining warehouses, but textiles were on the way out all over the state and the town was hard hit. The line was abandoned, the warehouses emptied. Now the only active warehouse held a children's discount furniture store.

Two years back, Allen Bates bought the tunnel; bricked off the front and back; added doors, electricity, plumbing, and ventilation; and brought the funky structure up to code. Now, on Friday and Saturday nights, the place was packed with local teens who danced under the spinning lights until the gray stone walls grew slick with their sweat.

Playing Tunnel Vision had been Torn's only goal for the six months they'd been together. Now they were here. So what bothered Devin?

Last gasp
Make it pound
Why are you still hanging 'round?

Maybe it was the song. Maybe deep down he thought "Face" sucked and sooner or later somebody would figure that out and call him on it. It had taken only ten minutes to write. That didn't bug Cody. Torn's totally psycho front man launched into his searing guitar solo with extreme gusto. The new axe sounded great, even if it was a complete mystery how someone as financially strapped as Cody could afford it.

Maybe Devin was just looking for something to be wrong. If he was, he found it. Just as the number was ending, Karston, their skinny, anxious, self-conscious bassist, lost his place. The crowd had already started applauding, so most likely no one in the audience noticed, but Cody did. He spun and gave the bassist a killing look with his bright green eyes.

Leave him alone! Devin thought, grinding his teeth, as if Cody could hear him. *The last thing we need is to make him more nervous!*

Before Cody could fire away with any more

laser-beam glances, Devin nodded at Cheryl and they launched into "If It Doesn't Kill You," Cody's song. It was a trick he and Cheryl used on Cody. Whenever he got out of line they'd hold up something bright and shiny to distract him. Sometimes Cheryl would flirt with Cody playfully; sometimes they'd go into a song. Devin and Cheryl were good together that way. In a lot of other ways, too.

Devin's chords blasted through the amp, rolling between A and F-sharp minor with a fast, easy rhythm. The crowd started up again, clapping to Cheryl's beat. Cody forgot Karston and went at the vocal with major passion.

For some incomprehensible reason, the incident made Devin relax a little, like it made everything seem more real. He even started enjoying himself during the last of Torn's three-number tryout set, "Flush with Your Foot." It was an early effort, stupid fun, written a year ago, when Devin was sixteen. Cody really let loose on that one, vamping up and down the stage, and in the end adding an outrageous, unexpected solo.

Which was not good. Unexpected things, that is. Not with Karston at the bass. He'd been doing better since his "Face" screw-up, but now lost it completely, hitting the wrong notes, off tempo. He sounded like an elephant with bad gas farting into a mike. Cody caught the mistakes just as he was going down on his knees in a dramatic stage move. Devin watched as Cody, in the middle of finishing his lick, tried twisting his head to give Karston another nasty look.

It wasn't pretty. The usually graceful frontman went off-balance, catching his bare shoulder on a jagged metal clip on the corner of his amp. Blood, looking black in the blue light, flowed freely down his long arm, spotting his shirt. It was a moment that could've spelled disaster. But it didn't.

The pain didn't stop or surprise Cody. It set him on fire. He went on with his solo for another eight bars, then finished as the crowd cheered wildly, not one of them caring about or remembering Karston's mistakes. They were all too busy watching Cody finally proving to himself and the world that he was the real thing.

Allen Bates beamed at them, his large hands again slapping together, this time loud enough to be heard over the crowd.

"Torn!" Bates screamed again. The band headed for the storage area behind the stage that passed for a dressing room. Devin knew—they all knew—from Bates's face they'd be invited back.

They'd done it. Now all they needed were enough songs to fill a twenty-minute set.

Once the door was closed, Cheryl flew into Devin's arms. Borrowing her enthusiasm, he swung her around, feeling the heat of her body against his.

"Yes, yes, yes!" she screamed. "It's like I'm dreaming and I don't want to wake up!"

She kissed him hard, finally giving him the buzz he'd craved from the crowd. He'd have to be dead not to react to her. Devin had never thought he'd have a chance with a girl as beautiful as Cheryl, and now they'd been seeing each other for three months. At first he used to get jealous when he saw how other guys looked at her, even Cody, but tonight he figured she was all his.

He stopped kissing her long enough to say, "Tomorrow!"

His parents had gone away for the weekend, and after Torn came over for some recording, he and Cheryl had a big night planned. Usually when they wanted to be alone, they had to head to an abandoned housing development near his home and park. Even the roomy seats of his Dad's SUV could be awkward in that situation, but tomorrow they'd have a whole big, empty house, at least from nine, when rehearsal ended, until

Cheryl's midnight curfew.

Cody strutted into the center of the room like a prize bull, ignoring them. He stretched his Les Paul high over his head and made a sound that could only rightly be described as a roar. Ben, also known as One Word Ben, since he seldom spoke, applauded. Even Karston grinned sheepishly.

"We are so damn cool!" Cody cried.

"Not that it's going to our head or anything," Devin said, still holding Cheryl aloft. She was so light, he felt like he could carry her forever.

Cody laughed. "Whatever. *I* am so damn cool! The rest of you suck!"

Everyone took it as a joke, until Cody glanced over at Karston and the gleam in his eyes shifted from glazed megalomania to something more predatory. Cody snarled and moved as if he were going to attack. Karston visibly shriveled.

Tensing, Devin reluctantly let Cheryl slide off his body, in case he had to pry Cody away from the smaller, thinner teen. Cody could be brilliant and exciting, but so could lightning. The singer had a penchant for explosive, demanding, infantile, and downright psychotic behavior. Devin looked around for another shiny object to distract him, to break the tension, when he noticed the blood still dripping down the side of Cody's arm.

"Going to do anything about that cut?" Devin asked, pointing.

Cody howled wildly, twisted his head, and licked the fresh blood off with his long tongue. "Yum!" he said, pleased with himself.

"Disgusting," Cheryl said, but she looked a little tickled.

"How would you know? You haven't tasted me yet," Cody answered. He wiped the cut with his broad, long-fingered hand, looked at it a moment and slapped Karston on the back.

A silence followed, during which Devin held his breath, but then Cody just said, "Come on, let's get some free food before the next band plays."

"Yeah!" said One Word Ben.

As they moved out, Cody pulled Devin back by the shoulder. "Hang back a minute."

Devin had his arm around Cheryl's waist and didn't want to let go. "Can it wait?"

"No."

Cheryl rolled her eyes and slipped out. Devin felt the warmth depart. The back room was cool and the sweat from the lights and the performance was drying on his skin. He got ready to launch into his usual speech about how hard Karston was trying, how he'd worked all summer saving every penny to buy that bass and amp, even if it was only a four-string knock-off, how he practiced for hours every day, and how hard it was to find a bassist in Macy, but Cody didn't let him. He just said:

"Karston's out and you have to tell him."

"What?"

"He's holding us back."

"Holding us back? We played one night here. It's not like we have a recording contract, or even more than three songs." Devin laughed.

Cody was dead serious. "Yeah, that's exactly it. We've only got three songs because that's all he can play. Do you know how much we can't do because of him? I had a solo worked out for a cover of 'Hey Bulldog' that would've kicked major ass, but he can't even handle the opening riff. He can't even play a stupid run from a third to a fifth to a seventh without thinking about it for twenty minutes."

There was a flat tone to Cody's voice that told Devin he'd already made up his mind, but Devin had to give it a shot anyway.

"He's trying, Cody, he's really trying."

"So what? He's not succeeding." He held the Les Paul out toward Devin. Its surface shone, even in the dim light. "Like the new axe? Nice, huh? I risked a lot for this guitar because I know we can make it. You heard them out there. If we could make a decent recording of 'Face,' we'd be getting local radio time, but we can't because Karston sucks."

Devin tried for something bright and shiny. "How *did* you pay for the axe?"

Cody would not be moved. "You don't want to know, and don't change the subject. You know I'm right. The only question is, when are you going to tell him?"

Devin's eyes flared. "Me? Why me?"

Cody snapped his fingers in front of Devin's face. "Because I could do it like that, just like I broke it off with my last girlfriend—what's her name?"

"Debbie."

"Whatever. But you're always straddling the fence like it's a hot girl. You never even would have asked Cheryl out if I hadn't threatened to tell her you were ready to stalk her. I could've had her, too, you know, but I didn't, as a favor to you. But your wussiness, man, it's in your face, it's in your voice, it's in your music, and if we're going to get

28

anywhere, it's time to step up! Testify!" Cody put his hand on Devin's shoulder. "Look, I'm only telling you what an asshole you are because I'm your friend. I don't want this to be a game anymore; I want it to be my life, and if you want something to be your life, you have to be willing to risk your life for it, right?"

Devin stood there, unable to speak. Cody shoved him gently backward, then headed for the door. "And you better get out of your lame moodiness and start writing more kick-ass songs, man. We're hot. People are watching. Time to stop being a poser."

The door opened and Cody disappeared into the light and sound beyond, leaving Devin among quiet crates and cardboard boxes. That feeling of not being quite a part of things came over him again, hard and heavy. He was watching himself, watching himself, watching.

Cody was right about Karston. Was he right about Devin? Cody was all fire. His father, a former textile worker, had been unemployed for years. Now Cody had a mean-streets rut to rebel against, and no future to look forward to except retail. What did Devin have to overcome? A comfy bourgeoisie life in a million-dollar pre-fab home, so cookie-cutter it was called a McMansion, with a flat-panel TV and Dad's SUV to truck the band around in? What was he? What was his life? Where was his fire?

No one's pure, my love …

What was that? A poem? A nursery rhyme? A song?

Oh yeah, the lullaby his grandma used to sing. It seemed to come out of nowhere to tickle the back of his head the way her hand used to. The few words and notes came to his mind easily, but the rest refused to form. There were angels in it and some kind of monster that took away bad kids. Bad kids like Cody. Was that why Devin was so lame? Because deep down he was still obeying his grandma? Ha.

The line tumbled about in his mind, repeating. Devin rolled it around his head, trying to imagine it with a backbeat. Then it was gone. He put aside the fractured bit of memory for later use, then tried to figure out just what it was he was going to tell Karston. Best to get it over with fast, if he could.

Sighing, he stepped out into the throbbing sounds of the dance floor. A DJ spun house music while the next band set up. As Devin walked along, some people he didn't know looked at him admiringly. An older girl, maybe a college girl, smiled at him hungrily.

So this is what it's like to be in the band. Cool.

He smiled back, bemused, detached, until Cheryl grabbed him by the arm and pulled him onto the dance floor.

As he danced with her, smelling the shampoo in her hair that mixed with the smell of her sweat, he cast some nervous glances in the direction of the soon-to-be-former bassist. Karston, of course, was having the best night of his pathetic life. It looked like any girl who couldn't get near Cody because he was flailing too wildly on the dance floor had zeroed in on One Word Ben and Karston. The poor guy looked awake and happy for the first time in his life, ever.

Devin couldn't knock him off his perch, not like that. He'd never have this much attention again. No one at Argus High even spoke to the guy. Even Devin only started talking to him because they were next to each other in Bio, and he felt bad for him. Then he made the stupid mistake of mentioning he wanted to start a band.

He couldn't fire him right now.

31

He caught a glimpse of Cody at one of the small tables, his hands moving quickly as he spoke to two older kids. They weren't from school, and they definitely weren't in college. Cody was sitting back in his chair, a stupid grin plastered across his face as the other two talked to him. He actually looked nervous. One kid was steady, too calm, like a statue. The other was tall, but there was something wrong with his shoulder. It kept twitching. When the twitchy figure tilted, the image of a razor on the back of his leather jacket came into view.

Cheryl noticed Devin stiffen. "What's the matter?"

The Slits. Cody was talking with two members of the worst street gang in Macy. They dealt drugs, ripped off stores at gunpoint, even got into a little loan-sharking.

Oh. Was *that* where Cody got the money for the new axe?

"Nothing," Devin said.

Couldn't be. Even Cody wasn't stupid enough to get involved with that crowd.

Was he?

If you want something to be your life, you have to be willing to risk your life for it, right?

Of course he was.

Moonlight flashed over Cody's bleached white hair and ruddy face as he curled up in the passenger seat like some exotic animal. Devin dutifully maneuvered the SUV on the thin road out of town toward the more rural area where Cody lived with his father, stepmother, and five brothers and sisters.

Devin stayed silent, hoping he could remain that way. After about ten minutes, a light rain started falling, misting the black finish on his lawyer-dad's SUV.

Finally, Cody said, "Didn't do it, did you?"

Devin shook his head. "It's a bad move. Where would we get another bassist?"

"Ben. We'll move him over from keyboards."

"He doesn't play bass."

"He will. And he'll be better than Karston. He's got all that stuff hardwired from those piano lessons Mommy forced him to take since he was five. Guy's a total robot, but he's our robot."

"And where are we going to get a bass?"

"Borrow Karston's. He's not going to be using it."

Devin's voice frog-hopped an octave. "You want me to fire him and ask him to borrow his bass? You psychotic bastard."

"I'm not a psycho, dude, I'm a sociopath. He'll do it. He'll do it just to be near us."

Devin shook his head. "I do not believe you. You are a piece of work, Cody. You know his mother's a major bitch on wheels—she's like Mrs. Hannibal Lecter, totally abusive. She screams at him. She hits him. We're all he's got."

Cody made a face. "Yeah, and my mom was an alcoholic before she slammed into a nice thick pine tree doing sixty on a side street. Boo hoo hoo. It doesn't change the facts. He can't play. You love him so much, get rich and then send him to freaking college, so he can learn a useful trade. We're either serious or this is a game. I'm serious. I'm waiting to find out where you are. So where are you?"

They were driving on a low road surrounded by thick forest. A small car zoomed up behind them and started tailgating. Devin could hear the steady boom-boom of its car speakers mix with the swish of his wipers.

"Damn," Devin said. The road was slick and he didn't want to speed up, so he pulled to the shoulder and let the car pass. Two girls gave him the finger as they drove by.

Cody laughed. "Big shot rock star!"

Devin had nothing to say to that.

When his laugh faded, Cody leaned his forehead against the window and looked out at the darkness flashing between the tall trees, uncharacteristically contemplative. He let out a deep sigh.

"Okay. I got kicked out of school," he said. "Permanently. I don't need it. I know where I'm going and it doesn't involve algebra."

Devin stared at him. Cody and Argus High were mortal enemies since the first time he walked through the front door metal detectors. A dozen possible scenarios for Cody's expulsion flashed in Devin's head.

"No way. Because of the fight you were in today? I heard you hit a teacher, but I figured that was B.S. Even you're not . . . ," Devin said. He let his voice trail off as he turned to his passenger.

Cody gave him a look. "I shoved a basketball jock with a big mouth into the soda machine and his lunch went all over the floor. Chunky Meat Stew Special. Same freaking color as the linoleum. Douchebag Skiffler made me help him pick it up. So, okay, I bent down and scooped the slop back onto the tray. I was handing it back to the lame a-hole, all nicey nice, when Skiffler put his hand on my shoulder and squeezed, like I'm supposed to be afraid of his wrinkled ass. And he said, 'Snap it up, Mr. Dosser, I've got better things to do with my time.'"

Cody paused. The wipers slapped the windshield clean. Then, beaming like he was that lame jock sinking a three-pointer, Cody grinned and clenched his fist. "I slammed that Chunky Meat Stew Special right in Skiffler's chest. 'Lick it up yourself,' I told him."

Devin's mouth dropped open.

Cody laughed hysterically, but the crazed pleasure soon disappeared from his face. "Got a call after school. I'm supposed to be all thankful he's not pressing assault charges."

For Devin, things clicked into place. The new

36

guitar, the desire to get rid of Karston and get more serious with the band. Torn really was all Cody had.

"What'd your folks say?" Devin asked.

Cody shrugged. "Haven't told them. I erased the machine, but I'll hear about it tonight. They're probably waiting for me, white-knuckling it in the living room."

A set of lights rode in the rainy gray behind them. At first Devin was afraid it was a second tail-gater, but the lights slowed at a respectful distance and kept pace.

"So this is it," Cody explained. "You want to get all weepy over Karston, go right ahead, but I can't screw around anymore. You either fire him before the recording session tomorrow, or *I'll* quit."

"Right."

"Try me," Cody said, a little angry. "I'll hitch into the city. I'm good enough to get session work. I'll pull another band together."

Cody leaned sideways and punched Devin's shoulder. "But I don't want to do that, man. I want it to be Torn. I want it to be us. I just need it to be *now*. 'Face' is an okay song—that and my vocal got us the gig. You've got something there. But you've

37

also got Daddy's kick-ass SUV and his giant bank account sending you to any college you want. I need to know where you're at with this and I need to know now."

So here it was.

Cody's life was on the brink, and he was all set, eager even, to take the plunge. Devin wished he felt the same, but if he put more time into the band, made it more than a hobby, how could he keep up his own schoolwork? Studying was the only thing that got him past half his classes. But he loved music, loved Torn. Wasn't the whole point of dreams to make them real?

The road narrowed. The trees grew taller. Moonlight poked from between the rain clouds, shone through the branches, reflected off the windshield, then vanished again. More time passed.

"How does that fence feel, shoved between your legs like that?" Cody asked. "You gonna answer? I'm not kidding. Karston goes and you tell him."

"I don't know," he said. "I just don't know."

The road curved into a fork. Devin took it a little fast, so he had to slow down to follow the line of the deserted street. As he did, he heard tires screech behind him.

What the hell?

Engine gunning, the car in the rear roared into the left lane, passed him, went fifty yards ahead, and then spun, blocking the road.

Devin's shocked mind seized, but his body managed to hit the brakes. The heavy SUV came to a wavering halt. Devin's body slammed forward from momentum, the hard edges of the seat and shoulder belt pressing into his skin.

The next thing he saw was Cody, ripping off his own belt in a panic, then nearly throwing himself into the back, pulling things from his bag, screaming, "Oh crap, oh crap, oh crap!"

Devin snapped forward, ready to rage at the stupid driver. Through the windshield he saw the doors of what looked like a dark sedan fly open. Into the headlights came the Slits he'd seen at Tunnel Vision, looking mean in leather jackets that glistened in the soft rain.

"So Cody," Devin said, his voice shaking, "is this where you got the money for the guitar?"

But "Oh crap, oh crap, oh crap" was Cody's only answer as he continued to rummage frantically. The Slits headed toward the SUV. Their legs moved, but it seemed like the rest of their bodies were motionless, making it look as if they weren't getting closer so much as growing larger.

Devin was staring so intensely, he was only dimly aware of Cody slipping back into the front seat. The feel of something cold and heavy in his lap brought his senses back to the cab. He looked down. A crowbar. Cody had tossed him a crowbar.

"No! No way!" Devin said. "Are you crazy? Are you totally crazy?"

"Take it!" Cody growled. "There's only two of them! We can scare them off!"

Devin pushed the crowbar back at Cody. "No! What happens next time when there's more than two?"

Cody slammed it back into Devin's hands and held it there. "Nick and Jake and their stupid pals are all talk. They're nothing. Nothing. The only reason they get away with this crap is because no one challenges them. They'll back off if we put up a fight, trust me. Follow my lead. They don't carry guns. It's all knives and razors. Crowbar's longer than a knife, right?"

The two figures approached, not even blinking from the rain. Devin briefly wondered which was Jake and which was Nick, then realized he didn't care. Cody shivered in a weird way, like he was trying to shake any fear out of his face.

He opened the door, hopped out, and cast an angry look back inside at Devin.

"Come on!"

Devin thought seriously about calling the cops, but the Slits could kill both of them in the time it would take a squad car to get here. He wanted to drive off, but Cody was already out of the car. So, gritting his teeth and trying to keep his terrified body in control, Devin stepped out of the SUV and stood on the other side.

Seeing him, the short one (Nick? Jake?) veered and took a step toward Devin, but the other stopped him. His hand sported a big, gaudy ring on a finger that looked more muscular than some arms. He jabbed it at Devin like a knife.

"Stay out of this. It's not your problem unless you want it to be," the Slit said. "You just stand there and watch."

When Devin didn't move or speak, the Slit turned to Cody. "We want our money."

"I told you back at the club, I haven't got it," Cody said. "I don't know when I will."

The Slit shook his head. "That's not good."

41

"No," Cody answered. "It's not."

The two took another step closer. Cody moved his feet apart for better balance. The change in stance only made the Slit with the twitchy shoulder grin. He took one more step. In a totally defensive move, born out of fear, Devin raised the crowbar slightly.

The taller Slit looked at him. "You seem like a good kid. Close your eyes if you don't want to watch. It won't take long. That way you'll still be conscious, so you can drive your friend to the hospital."

"Put that crowbar through his skull, Devin," Cody said.

"Aren't you already in enough trouble?" the Slit asked.

"See?" Cody said, not taking his eyes from the Slit. "I told you they're all talk."

The taller Slit took a step toward Devin. His eyes were calm. Blank. All business. Devin felt his grip on the crowbar weaken, his shoulders slump. He moved his hand to wipe the moist rain from his eyes.

"Come on, Devin!" Cody said. "Gotta get off that fence sometime. Now would be good."

"Yeah, Devin, what's it going to be? I don't have all night," the Slit said, grinning.

In a flash, the grin vanished. Something hit him hard from the side, sending the Slit down and out of Devin's field of vision. Devin turned, confused. Cody was down on the Slit, pummeling him, hitting him again and again in the face and the chest, really wailing on him.

The twitchy Slit was stunned by the sudden attack, but recovering. Any second, he'd jump Cody and it'd be two-on-one.

Whatever happened next was up to Devin. But why? How far was friendship supposed to go? If crazy Cody was stupid enough to borrow money from thugs, why should Devin risk his neck?

"Devin! Do *something*!" Cody shouted between blows. The Slit below him tried to block the manic flurry of punches, but Cody was too fast.

The other Slit shifted.

The car door was less than a foot away. Devin could get in quickly, then wait and watch. Like he always did.

"Devin!" Cody bellowed. He turned his head. When he did, the Slit landed a blow to the side of his face. Cody was mean and fast, but no street

43

fighter and not very heavy. He went sideways. In seconds, the two reversed positions, the Slit on top, ready to get medieval.

Shaking, frightened, Devin tightened his grip and held the crowbar up, hoping he could have it both ways and scare them off without actually doing anything. He took a step, but his foot found something slick on the rain-wet road. His foot flew back and he flew forward.

The shorter Slit raised his arm as the crowbar came down. It hit him in the center of his forearm, with all Devin's falling weight behind it. There was a loud sound, a crack like a thick branch splitting. Devin hit the ground and ate some street. Badly scraped, he managed to stumble back to standing in time to still see the look of surprise on the Slit's face.

A voice in the back of Devin's brain said, *Did I hurt him?*

Numbly, he raised the crowbar again. The Slit, arm folded in a funny way, moved back. Devin turned toward the one atop Cody. The cracking sound had turned him around, too, long enough for Cody to pull back and slam him full on in the crotch.

In pain, the Slit moved sideways a bit and snarled. The mask of calm he'd worn previously vanished, revealing something savage and animal.

Moving like a caffeinated maniac, Cody rolled out and up onto the balls of his feet. The Slit, grabbing his crotch, looked around and saw his partner cradling his arm and moaning. He stumbled back to their car, pulling his friend along. Just before he vanished into the driver's side, he said, "This isn't over."

With a squeal of tires on the wet asphalt, the small car spun and zoomed off into the darkness.

Devin watched it go, catching his breath a moment. He turned back to Cody, who was laughing, harder and harder, and saying, "That was great! That was amazing! We are Torn!"

Devin looked at him, shocked. How could he be laughing? What could be more stupid?

Then he started laughing himself. He was relieved. Happy, like he'd won something, like maybe, even though it was an accident, even though he hadn't really decided anything, he was now bad enough to be in a rock and roll band.

Hours later, Devin McCloud lay in his comfortable bedroom, waiting for sunrise. The house was quiet, his parents fast asleep. He was exhausted. By rights he should have been unconscious, but his brain was locked—and not on Cody and the Slits. Though the nervous energy that propelled his thoughts was probably a leftover from that encounter, his focus was on the fact that Torn was getting together in less than twelve hours to record "Face" in Devin's garage, and sometime before then, he would have to fire Karston.

Grateful though Cody had seemed because Devin had fought by his side, he had not given up on that point. Karston's bass was supposed to be there; Karston was not.

When the Slits had fled, Devin had felt exhilarated. Now he just felt tired and kind of sick. Shifting up onto his elbow on the soft mattress, he stared out his large round window at the manicured lawns and squared hedges of the gated Meadowcrest Farms housing development. As far as he could tell, the development had nothing to do with a meadow, a crest, or a farm. It had more to do with tiny, well-tended yards, and neighbors who seemed to pose as they stopped and smiled and waved. The squares, rectangles, and circles that made up the houses were tight and perfect. Everything seemed held together by money.

But even in the dim light of early morning, Devin could see exactly where the lawn mowers and hedge clippers stopped and something else began, something jagged and unkempt: a dark forest that went on for miles. As a child he hadn't been allowed to go in there; now he just didn't want to, as if all the years of comfort and security had left him too comfortable and secure.

He wasn't like Cody. He wasn't a natural. He wasn't driven. He wasn't sure. He didn't even know if he could write any decent songs. What was "Face," anyway? What did it mean?

As his eyes half closed, a line from the lullaby

drifted back to him. It was his grandma's song; Namana, he used to call her.

Your heart beats slowly, drowsy eyes...

It was a pretty thing, the tune. Even the small bit playing in his mind relaxed him. The rest of the words and the melody licked at the edge of memory, teasing, just out of reach, like the woods. As he reached for more words with his mind, they dissipated, like ghosts.

Half awake, he found that strong images came to him more easily. He remembered being curled up deliciously cozy in Namana's lap when she babysat. There was a stuffed toy in his hand. When she started singing, he'd bury his head in the toy, hide in its darkness until he felt drowsy. He could feel the rough fur against his cheek, hear her old voice as she croaked more than sang.

Or else the wild will come for you.

And snatch bad children away? A tingling along his spine told him he was on the right track.

Be good or *else*.

By the time he was six, his mother said, he had demanded Namana never sing it again. It was too horrible—he thought it might be real, that something might really come and kill him. Stupid. But at six, you think everything might be real, everything except real-life horrors like the Slits.

Be good or *else*.

Funny, but weren't all the lullabies and nursery rhymes like that? Lost children, cannibalistic witches? Didn't the famous ones talk about dying before you wake, or a baby falling screaming out of a treetop? Wasn't ring-around-the-rosy about the black plague? The symptoms and the fatal sneezing fit were wrapped into the cute lyrics:

Achoo! Achoo! We all fall down!

As if they were waiting for just the right moment, a few more strands of the lullaby came back. They gave him a rush more familiar than the adrenaline frenzy of his fight. This was the kind of rush that came when something inside of him filled him up to bursting, the kind he got whenever he was trying to write a song and he was on to something. This was something.

Your heart beats slowly, drowsy eyes ...

Devin thought maybe he could call Namana, visit her, ask her how it really went. The senior care facility was just an hour away. She'd love it. No one ever visited. But no. He didn't want to deal with that place, or with her being old and feeble. The last time she hugged him (two years ago at Christmas?) her hands and arms felt so thin against his neck, it was like being grabbed by a skeleton.

Besides, it would ruin it if he knew the real song. This was better. The less perfectly Devin remembered it, the more he was free to make it his own.

He snapped on the light by his bed, plugged in his amp, slipped on his headphones, and played, fumbling around for the right notes, finding them more and more often. He paused occasionally, scratched down some chord progressions with the nub of a pencil, crossed others out, and filled in the missing parts with his own inventions.

As he worked, it came to him faster, as if he were in a welcome trance. Sitting there, sleepless, working on a dream, reminded him why he'd helped Cody form Torn in the first place, why he was so worried about not being worthy. Because sometimes, like right now, working on the music made him forget all the hesitancy, all the guilt, all the fence-straddling.

In an hour, he was finished, and he liked it. It wasn't like "Face" or any of his other songs. This was soft, but it had something edgy to it, too. Cody's voice alone could make it ache. And when he imagined Cody singing, Cheryl on drums, him on rhythm, and Ben on bass, it made Devin feel more than real; it made him feel like he was on fire.

A little giddy, he sang it to himself, in his head so as not to wake his parents, to make sure it all worked. As he sang, a chill went up his spine and settled heavily on his shoulders—as if there were suddenly something right behind him, something thick and dangerous. The feeling was so strong, so pointed, he even stood up and stared out his window.

As he scanned the line where the woods began, he thought he saw something move, but it was only shadow bumping into shadow as the wind twisted the branches of the trees.

He laughed as he realized he'd spooked himself. He'd written a song that actually spooked him!

Was that cool, or what?

Now all he had to do was fire Karston.

Saturday had arrived in earnest. With only a few hours' sleep behind him, a resolute Devin drove the good-old monster SUV across the abandoned tracks into Karston's lower-class neighborhood. As he did, he was struck by how everything here seemed held together by wood—old rotting wood that was frayed at the edges, badly painted, and ready to give. Things were shaped like houses and stores, but really they looked like they were ready to call it quits and go back to being forest.

Despite his resolve, driving slowly in the huge car Devin again felt undeserving, conspicuous, and after the Slit attack, unsafe. He also felt annoyed with himself for feeling all of the above. He'd driven here before without any problems, but today everything seemed sharp and pointy, like it was ready to cut him.

It was probably just the lack of sleep.

The block that held the shotgun shack the bassist occupied with his single mom was easy to find; there was an old refrigerator on the corner that no one ever bothered to clear away. It just sat there as if waiting for the bus. The door was missing, so there was a clear view of the brownish stains inside that may once have been some sort of food.

After making the turn, Devin parked in front of a garbage-strewn lot across the street. Before popping open the door and getting out, he gave himself a moment to chill. He looked at his oblong face in the rearview mirror, examining the bump in the center of his nose that his mother suggested he have removed when he was older. His light brown hair looked stiff and stringy. Pleased by how much stubble he had on his face, he rubbed it thoughtfully. The little garnet earring in his upper right ear always looked weird to him, but it, and the piercing, were a gift from Cheryl.

He realized he looked like he felt: terrible. But what did that matter? It was time to do the deed.

Cody could be a crazy son of a bitch, but he was right. Devin really did need to do this. Karston, in the end, would be better off finding out sooner rather than later that he didn't have what it takes . . . right?

Still looking at himself, he remembered something Samurai warriors did before going off into battle. They would look at themselves, then make some sort of ridiculous face to distract their minds. Following suit, Devin stuck his tongue out at himself, then hopped from the driver's seat and punched the Lock button on the keys.

The avenue was quiet, since most folks were sleeping off Friday night, so the chirp of the locking car seemed horribly loud. He winced at the sound, but no one else seemed to have heard.

His sneakers crunched along the decaying asphalt as he approached the chain-link fence. Its silver paint bubbled in spots and the poles were marred by reddish rust. Stalky dead plant-things stuck out along the bottom of the fence, threatening to claim the sidewalk. On the other side, a gray walk led to wooden stairs and a porch littered with beer bottles, most empty, some stuffed with cigarette butts.

He would do it, Devin thought; he would get it over with now. He thought about buying himself a new DVD as a reward, but just before his foot hit the first step, he heard shouting.

"I just can't believe what an idiot you are! How old are you? When are you going to grow up? You're wasting your life hanging out with crooks and sluts!"

Devin knew the voice. It came from Karston's mother, a short, pit bull of a woman. She had a kind of back-of-the-throat dying-animal screech that brought up phlegm at the end of every sentence. Even when she was saying something nice, like asking Devin if he wanted some water, you could hear the hate.

"I keep telling you I was with the band! We played at a club! We were really good!" This was Karston. His voice had volume, too, but there was no anger, only a wimpy, surrendering tone.

"Did they pay you?"

"A little."

Even though he was outside, with the walls of a house between them and no windows open, Devin could hear her disapproving "Tch."

More whining from Karston: "They invited us back next week to play a full set. I'm recording with the group this afternoon!"

"Recording, right. Makes me sick, all that money you wasted and you can't even keep that thing in tune. Watch. The two crooks and the slut will dump you first chance they get, just as soon as they can get that bass away from you. That's all they want."

Devin felt something in his gut tighten. It was true. Except the slut part.

A long pause followed, as if Karston were considering. Finally, he said, "No. Devin would never do that."

Great. *Devin* would never do that. Cody would. Cody would do anything. But not Devin. He was the nice guy. The good kid. The knot in Devin's gut twisted.

"Oh, Devin! Devin, Devin, Devin. You trust that spoiled brat?" the shrill voice shouted. "You're going to wind up just like your father!"

For the first time, anger appeared in Karston's voice. "Keep my father out of this!"

Frozen at the rusted gate, Devin heard footsteps moving on a wooden floor. The next sound was a hard slap of skin against skin, followed by Karston's whiny, "Ahh! Don't hit me!"

That was it. Devin turned around, got back in his father's car, drove home, and spent the rest of the afternoon fiddling with the melody to his new song, trying to get it just right, wondering if it would ever be bright and shiny enough to distract the adamant Cody, if only for a little while.

Once Devin's parents gave him the long list of warnings for his weekend home alone, declared their faith in his maturity, and finally left, the afternoon slipped by quickly and the time for the recording session neared.

Karston, of course, showed up first. It was a mystery how he got around, but he always showed up and never dared ask anyone for a ride. Speculation was that he hitched, or took some bizarre combination of public transport. After exchanging hellos, Devin explained that he had to pick up some soda and left the bassist alone in the garage.

By the time Devin returned, Cheryl was there.

She had her own car, and had driven over from the nearby development where she lived. As he stepped back in, she looked up from her half-assembled drum kit, made a face, and said, "You look different."

Before he could begin to wonder what she meant, Cheryl stepped out from behind the drums and walked closer, filling Devin's field of vision with smooth, beautiful skin, straight blond hair, and natural energy. By the time she stopped coming closer, he had a good view of the faint freckles on her cheeks.

What could it be? Had his encounter with the Slits magically matured him overnight? Was it finally writing a song he felt good about? Or both?

Whatever it was, she scanned his face, brow furrowed. "You look more . . . rugged," she finally said. Her eyes continued their investigation, questioning his features, focusing on his lips. "Reminds me of someone. Cody?"

He frowned, so she went up on tiptoes to kiss him. "Mmm. Nice mix. Sexy."

He was going to grab and kiss her again when he caught a glimpse of Karston over her head. His eyes were hidden by dangling hair, but he was watching. Remembering they weren't quite alone, Devin stepped back and smiled. "Maybe I'm just excited about tonight," he said.

Cheryl shook her head slowly. "No. That's not it. Did something happen?"

"Yeah," he said in a low voice. "Tell you later."

"Let's get this party started," Cody howled as he and One Word Ben walked in. For a second, Devin hoped Cody had forgotten about Karston, or at least was willing to let it go for one night. But when Cody spotted Karston, he spun and glared at Devin with a malevolent twinkle in his eyes. His voice was flat and earnest as he said, "But first, Little Devin's got something very special to say to K—"

Before Cody could complete the name, Devin held up his hand. "Yeah. Yeah, I do have something to say."

And then Devin went silent.

"What?" said One Word Ben.

Good question, Devin thought. He turned to look at Karston. He was already bracing himself, already expecting something was up.

"I . . . I've got a new song I want you all to hear," Devin said. Now was as good a time as any, so he pulled up his acoustic Ovation, sat on a stool, checked the tuning, and started to play.

Sun is low, the sky gray, gray, gray,
All day's colors gone,
Your heart beats slowly, drowsy eyes,
Soon your dreams will come.

Don't start, sweet child, lay still, still, still.
Angels on their way
Will ride the breeze tonight to ask
If you were good today.

And when they do, say yes, yes, yes,
Even if you lie,
Or else the wild will come for you
And you will surely die.

It won't care how you cry, cry, cry,
Or swear how much you'll change.
It hasn't eaten for so long
Its stomach aches with rage.

No one's pure, my love, love, love,
But if you cross the line,

Your deeds will call out to the wild,
And there won't be much time.

So lay your head down, rest, rest, rest,
And when the angels ask,
Tell them just how good you've been
As long as the darkness lasts.

The last finger-picked notes from the guitar reverberated against the cinder-block walls of the two-car garage. As the echo melted away, Devin slipped the Ovation from his arms and leaned it against the stool. He cupped his hands in his lap and watched and waited. It was a risk playing anything on acoustic in front of Cody, but he wanted to sing it in a range his own voice could barely touch, and the softer guitar sound let his weaker vocal come through more clearly.

The late afternoon sun was just above the tree line outside the open garage door, making Devin's band-mates appear in silhouette. They just stood there a little while, looking at him, but he couldn't see any expressions on their faces.

Finally Cheryl held up her hand. "Wait," she said, then ran out.

In her absence, Cody twisted his head to the side in a kind of apelike way. "It's a ballad," he huffed.

"So?" said One Word Ben.

Karston shifted his position so he was standing nearly behind Devin. It was as if he was aware something was up and sought protection. Cody looked like he was about to say something when Cheryl raced back in, her camcorder in hand.

"Okay," she said, putting the viewfinder to her eye. "Play it again. Just the same way."

Devin looked at her. "On tape? Why?"

"I want a recording of our first hit song."

Devin laughed, figuring she was joking, but when not even Cody said anything, he did as asked and ran the song again, screwing up some of the picking in the middle as he became too aware of the camera.

When he was done, Cody said, "It needs a chorus."

Cheryl shook her head. "It's amazing."

"I didn't say it was bad or good. I said it needs a chorus."

But does Cody like it? Devin wondered. They needed more songs if they were going to fill a set, and Devin was confident this was as good as any they had, even if it wasn't exactly nu-metal. Had it worked as a distraction, though? Would Cody give Karston another night?

Cody lifted the strap of his Les Paul over his shoulder, but he still wasn't giving anything away. As he plugged into an amp and started tuning, he said, "We've only got until nine because of your big bad date, right, sweetie pie? Can we get started with the recording?"

Phew!

He'd gotten away with it, for the night anyway. Now it was up to Karston to make it through the recording session. Relieved, Devin flipped the switch that closed the garage door, and they got to it.

It was Torn's first effort at recording tracks. The method was twenty-first-century crude. Devin had downloaded a mixing program called Track It! for thirty bucks. It would supposedly let them lay down as many different tracks as his laptop's memory could hold. Then they'd mix down and convert the file to the coveted MP3, which Cheryl, Torn's webmistress, could upload to their site.

As they worked, the thought of the kids at Argus High School bopping with "Face" in their earbuds got Devin even more excited. With Karston and the new song on hold at least for the moment, they ran through "Face" twice, then recorded it whole hog through a single mike plugged into his laptop. The idea was that then they'd play individually, listening to the control track through the phones. That would give them one instrument or vocal per track, which they could mix to their heart's content.

As for Karston, maybe his mother's tongue-lashing had set him straight, because he played through the song all three times flawlessly, or as close to that as he could come. It was always a little easier for him during rehearsal, when he was free to stare down at his fingers the whole time.

As the evening progressed, Devin was thinking that not only had he dodged a bullet, they'd also be finished in plenty of time for his big date with Cheryl. With his folks gone, the band had agreed to split up at nine, to leave the two alone.

But then a technical problem set in. The laptop, wicked cool though it was, couldn't play back more than four tracks at a time without losing synch, freezing, or crashing. Thinking fast, Devin decided they could mix down the rhythm and drums, add two more tracks, mix them down and so on. It was even cruder than they'd planned, but it could work.

Cheryl and One Word Ben were naturals, knocking out their parts in two takes. Taking this as a challenge, Cody put down a lead in one. It was nothing like what he'd ever played before on the song, but it was great. It was like the guy hated playing the same thing twice.

"Now the bass," Cody said with a nearly imperceptible sneer.

"No," Devin said. "I'll have to mess with the equalizer to get a decent bass sound. How about vocals? With the vocals the settings are practically there already."

He could see an evil twinkle in Cody's eye. "You're the techno-geek."

The lead vocal was fine in the first take, but Cody insisted on two more, which brought them right up against the nine o'clock deadline with just the harmonies and the bass track to go.

Devin looked at the clock. "And that is time."

Everyone moaned. Cheryl sighed.

"Dev," she said sweetly, "nine thirty is just as good as nine for us, isn't it?"

But Devin was thrilled to have an excuse for separating Cody and Karston. He shook his head. "No, no. Time to pack it in. Karston can come back and add the bass tomorrow."

Which will be perfect, Devin figured. Alone, Karston could stare at his fingers, pick his nose, sacrifice to Zeus, whatever, and he wouldn't have Cody breathing down his neck. But more moans and groans issued forth. Even Karston opened his mouth. "Come on, Devin, I can do it. I feel really on tonight."

Sheesh! Don't you know when to shut up?

"Yeah," Cody echoed with more than a little sarcasm. "Karston is so on."

"Finish," One Word Ben chimed in.

Devin shook his head and started shutting down the laptop. "Deal's a deal." He was a little hurt that Cheryl didn't seem as eager as he was to be alone. But what came next made him feel better.

"Don't worry boys, I'll handle this," Cheryl said. She'd dressed in an orange blouse he'd always liked that showed some of her cleavage, and a tight pair of low-cut jeans. As Devin idly clicked a few laptop keys, she walked up, twisted him around, and pressed her lips against his. He felt her tongue poking at the ridge of his teeth in a way that made his head explode.

She pulled back and said again, just as sweetly, "Dev, nine thirty is just as good as nine, isn't it?"

"Nine thirty is the most amazing thing in the whole world," Devin answered dreamily. "It's my favorite time ever."

Devin moved to kiss her again, but she pulled away. Cody gave her a wicked smile.

"Okay," Devin said, surrendering. "How about this? We'll finish recording tonight and mix tomorrow. Why don't we pack up Cody and Ben and they can take off. You're driving Cody back, right Ben?"

"Right."

"Cool. Then Cheryl and I will finish recording Karston. Deal?"

Cody gave Devin another knowing look, but Devin just shrugged in response. Still staring at Devin, he unplugged his axe and moved to put it in the case.

"Dev," Cody said, too sweetly, "can you help me load up the amp?"

As they walked toward Ben's minivan, out of

earshot of the garage, Cody shook his head. "You get one extra night, that's all, and it's just delaying the inevitable, man. He's killing us."

"It'll be fine," Devin insisted.

"Don't think I won't know it if you play the bass for him," Cody said as he slipped his guitar case into the back.

"It'll be fine. Come on, you owe me for helping you with the Slits," Devin said.

Cody chuckled. "More like you owe me. It's the first thing you ever did with your life."

The words stuck in Devin's head as he watched them drive off toward the setting sun. He even waited until they were out of sight before heading back to the garage, fearful Cody might change his mind and come back.

When he finally did return to the ad-hoc studio, quiet, hesitant bass notes filled the air. Karston was deeper in the garage, by the hanging tools near the steel door that led to the house's interior. He was staring down at his shaking hands as he played his cheap bass.

In the few seconds it had taken Cody and Ben to pack up and leave, Karston's playing had grown much worse.

Devin raised his voice. "One take, right Karston? You're in the zone?"

"Yeah," Karston said, nodding enthusiastically.

How long can it last? Half an hour? Devin thought as he clicked the keys on his laptop. *It's simple. It's quiet. He's already run it three times. Then it's just me and Cheryl.*

He turned to Karston with a reassuring smile. In a week, "Face" would be burning its way through the school, then maybe the town. And his new one was even better, more real.

Despite the attack, it was turning out to be a great night.

What could possibly go wrong?

Hours later, the moonlight had long gone and Cheryl, her curfew approaching, was looking half asleep. Devin found his brain echoing the screech of Karston's mother, wishing the inept bass player had never bought the bass in the first place.

"Take it nice and easy, Karston," he said, trying really hard to keep his voice calm. "Listen to the control track. Give it a count of four . . . no, you know what, forget that. You just pick a beat, any beat you want, and start playing. Just play. And don't stop. You can do it, man."

Karston nodded. He nodded just like he'd nodded for the last ten takes he'd screwed up. But maybe, maybe even if Karston started early, or late, or in the middle, Devin could slide the track along on the laptop screen and synch it up. All he had to do was play the right notes and the right tempo. In fact, Karston didn't even have to play the whole damn song. If he just got one verse and one chorus, Devin could cut and paste that part of the track over like text in a word processor, and use it to fill in the rest of the song.

Boom-dah-bom-dah-boom. The low sound filled the garage.

Three notes, four . . . Devin counted, nodding his head in time. On the fifth, Karston hesitated, then stopped completely. It would probably be faster to record the bass line one note at a time.

"I'm sorry, man," Karston said, shaking his head.

It had been like this all night. Maybe Devin had been wrong to get Cody out of there. When they'd started, Karston was in the zone for three runs.

The zone? Ha. Who was Devin kidding? The only zone Karston was ever in was the Twilight Zone.

Devin removed his phones and tried to look at the clock on the wall without Karston realizing what he was doing. Almost eleven. Cheryl's parents were cool about her curfew, but even they weren't going to let her stay out all night.

"Karston, what is it? You were doing great. What's going on with you?" Devin asked. He was trying to sound friendly, but couldn't quite hide the anger in his voice. He even wondered, briefly, if as his patience vanished he was starting to sound more like Cody.

The bass player shrugged. "I don't know. It's just gone. I think maybe it's too quiet. I can like hear the houses and I'm afraid I'm waking people up."

Aghhh! It's too loud, it's too quiet. And I thought Cody was the group prima donna!

"There's no amp!" Devin said loudly. He battled his voice back down to a whisper. "It's just in the phones! No one can hear you except you and me."

"I know, but you know, psychologically . . ."

Psychologically? Now we're talking psychological? Should he tell him? Should he just say, *You know, Cody's dying to kick you out and I've been protecting you. You blow this simple stupid bass line again and I'm switching sides.*

Yeah, that'd give Karston the confidence he needed.

"Okay, once more. Take a breath. I'll cut out the keyboard and the vocal. Just listen to me and

72

Cheryl on the rhythm and drums. Got it?"

Karston nodded. Devin clicked a button, then said, "Go."

Karston bopped his head a few times, roughly in time. Devin watched as his fingers made for the first thick string. Then all of a sudden Karston stopped, shook his head, and pulled his head-phones off.

"I need a break," Karston said. "Is there any soda left?"

A break? You haven't laid down a single note! Devin's mind screamed, but he said, "Yeah, in the fridge. Bring me a cherry coke. Want anything, Cheryl?"

Cheryl swiped some hair and a bit of sleep from her eyes with her fingers and shook her head. She waited until Karston disappeared into the house, then said, "I'm exhausted, Devin. Sorry, but I've got to get going."

"What? But . . . but . . ."

She slid off the stool she'd been on for the last half hour. "I know, baby, I know. But this is more important for you—for all of us. Got to get the song done. We all want it out there before our next gig."

"No. It's not more important. Don't I ever get to

73

decide what's more important?" Devin protested. He stood up and made some vague gestures of frustration with his hands. She took them in hers and steadied them.

"It'll go faster without me here. We'll make up for it. Promise. Kiss good-bye?"

He grabbed her, pulled her close, and pretended he was just going to give her a quick peck, but then he moved back, stared into her eyes a moment, and slowly moved back in, brushing his lips against hers, back and forth, like a feather, then pressing in.

If she hesitated, he didn't notice. He put his arms around her waist, lifted her off the ground and even closer to him. She wrapped her legs around his thighs, making herself lighter, and gave in to his frustration for a moment or two. When they heard something shift in the kitchen on the other side of the wall, she hopped down and pulled herself away.

"No," she said.

"Yes," he said. It was more a plea than a command.

She laughed and pulled herself away. "No. Now, be nice to Karston."

Devin let out a low moan. "I won't."

"Yes, you will. You're a good guy. Stop pouting," she said at the garage door. "I'm not going any-where. Even with your weird new smile."

He grinned at that. "Okay. Want me to drive you?"

"And do what with my car? It's less than a mile. I'm just going to head in, watch the tape of my boyfriend playing his great new song, then go to sleep. Hey, if you want me so much, write us a song about it."

"You got it."

"Nothing I can't play for my mother."

"I'll try. But it won't be easy," he said.

She smiled, waved, and walked off toward her two-seat Civic. He heard her car engine start just as Karston—wussy, lame, infuriating, date-ruining Karston—emerged from the house. Once he heard her drive off, he pressed the button on the garage door and the hum of its closing sealed them off from the night.

"Okay, Karston," Devin said with a sigh. "Let's try it again."

By one thirty A.M., all the energy from the earlier, successful portion of the recording session had fled Devin. And Karston hadn't gotten any better. If possible, he was getting worse.

Devin pulled off his headphone and rubbed his temples.

"Maybe we should try again tomorrow?" Karston said hopefully.

With another bassist.

He should just tell him, get it over with, let him run home to his evil bat shrew of a mother and get used to a life retailing at Wal-Mart, where the cash registers practically operated themselves.

You wasted all your money on that stupid bass!

A thought struck him. "Karston, wait here a minute. I'm gonna . . . I'm gonna try to think a minute about what to do here."

Karston nodded as Devin headed for the door.

He hit a few more off-notes: *budda, bahh, thung.*

Devin stopped in his tracks and shook his head. "No—don't play, don't practice. Just . . . just sit there a minute, will you?"

"Okay," Karston said. Devin saw from the way his head went down that he suspected something was up. He had to tell him, and he had to tell him

76

now. But he had an idea that might make it go down just a little easier.

He went through the door and closed it behind him, which left him in the small hallway that led into the kitchen. The lights were all off, but the drapes and shades were wide open, leaving the sharp corners and rounded counters of the kitchen bathed in the bug-yellow of the Meadowcrest streetlights. Twin candles sat on the breakfast table in the dining room nook, a reminder of the great romantic evening that might have been. Two filet mignon steaks were still on the counter, bits of blood from the cellophane pooling onto the blue and white dish below it.

Devin shook his head and picked up the dish. He cursed to himself as some of the blood sloshed out of the plate and onto the floor. What else could go wrong? He put the dish in the fridge and looked around for something to mop up the stain. When no sponge or rag appeared to his eyes, his tiredness got to him. Angry, he stomped his foot down into the largest drop of steak blood, grinding it into the tile with his toe.

When even the pleasure of that fled, he pulled out a few paper towels, wet them, and dealt with the mess.

It was time to deal with the other mess now: Karston.

His idea was this: His parents had left him two hundred dollars cash in a small envelope on the kitchen desk for expenses and "emergency" money. He'd tell Karston he was out of the band, but then give him the money as a down payment for the bass. That way, at least, he wouldn't be out all his money, and the bass would stay behind. Devin might still be able to finish the song himself tonight. Maybe he and Cheryl could get together tomorrow afternoon, before his folks returned.

Tired though, he couldn't make out in the near dark the white envelope they'd left him on the desk, so he flipped the light on. It was there, shoved under an old *Pennysaver*.

He counted the bills and stiffened. Forty bucks were missing, and he hadn't touched the envelope since his father had given it to him. Someone had taken it. No one else had been in the house today. The doors were locked. That only left the band.

Cody needed money. Would forty bucks have made that much of a difference to him? Maybe. One Word Ben was so into his Christianity the guy never even lied. Cheryl was out of the question. Karston?

Devin stormed back to the door, opened it, and stood half in the kitchen, half in the garage. He knew his face was full of suspicion, but he didn't care.

"Karston? Did you see an envelope on the desk in the kitchen?"

Devin didn't have to say another word. Karston picked his head up, eyes wide open like a deer caught in headlights. At first he shook his head no, but then his eyes started darting back and forth. He scowled, then scrunched up his face like he was going to cry or something. Finally his head went back down and he sort of slithered off the stool and put a hand slowly, deeply, into his front pocket and withdrew two twenties.

"I'm sorry. I'm really sorry, Devin," Karston said, holding it out. "I was going to use it for some lessons."

Devin felt sheer rage explode in his gut. It rose into his chest, rippled out into his head and arms. He was going to start screaming, tell that stupid son of a bitch exactly what he thought of him, tell him about all the times he'd stood up for him, how tonight he'd ruined things with Cheryl for his sake, then kick his sorry ass out of the band, out of his house and into the street where he just didn't care what would happen to him.

The first in a long torrent of abusive, ugly words was about to erupt from Devin's mouth when . . .

WHUNK!

Something heavy slammed into the garage door so fast and loud it made them both leap a foot.

"What the hell was that?" Devin said, taking a step forward.

In a flash, Karston was on his feet and next to Devin. "An animal?"

Devin shrugged. "Squirrels and raccoons come for the trash sometimes, but nothing that . . ."

WHUNK!

The garage door rattled visibly. It looked like some of the vinyl slats had actually bent from the force of the blow.

And then, all the lights went out.

"Okay, so maybe not a squirrel," Devin said softly.

The garage door rattled again, but this time it wasn't a short, sudden noise. The white slats kept shaking, first the ones low to the ground, then higher and higher, making a more and more awful racket with each slat. After reaching eight feet, where the door met the ceiling, the shaking stopped.

"Crap, how tall is this thing?" Karston whispered.

Devin, more familiar with the sounds of his home, shook his head. "It's not tall. It's climbing."

There was a bit of a creak, then a light thud, like a jumping child or small man landing. A skittering went across the roof, sounding like long nails scraping against the tiles. Devin and Karston looked up into the darkness, trying to follow with their eyes. It slowed, tapped lightly, rushed to the far end of the garage roof, which connected to the rest of the house, then fell silent again.

"Call someone," Karston said.

"No," Devin said, making a face. "It's just an animal. Raccoons can get pretty huge. And the lights . . ."

A vaguely muffled explosion of splintering glass issued from above. Whatever it was, it had smashed a window.

Not an animal.

The rush of fear hit Devin hard and fast. It was stronger even than it had been when the car had cut him off in the road. This felt as if something in his chest had grabbed his heart and was trying to force it out of his mouth.

Human?

"This isn't over."

Could it be the Slits? Had they followed him?

Above and deeper inside the house, it sounded like the furniture was being pushed around in the master bedroom suite.

"It's inside," Karston squealed, his thin voice whiny and afraid.

The racket in the master bedroom grew. More things were being thrown around, as if in a rage. Devin wondered how he would explain the mess to his parents, then realized what a stupid worry that was right now.

Could Cody be playing some kind of sick joke? No. The Slits. It had to be. They were making some kind of point, taking revenge for messing with them. Even though he was still very much afraid, the thought focused Devin, made him angry. All he had to do was call the police. Response time for the local cops to get to Meadowcrest Farms was like two seconds. They'd show up in force and arrest all their criminal asses. There were advantages to having money.

Devin slapped his side, fingers feeling for his cell phone, then he remembered he'd left it outside in the car.

"Give me your cell," Devin hissed, turning to Karston.

Karston looked at him like he was nuts. "I don't have a cell phone."

Right. In addition to all his other attractive

qualities, Karston was also one of the only kids in Argus High School who didn't have a phone.

A loud bang from above made Karston shake worse than the garage door had. "What is that? I'm starting to freak," he said loudly.

Devin grimaced and spoke quietly. "Shh! Calm down. Stay quiet. The stupid genius Cody borrowed money from the Slits for his new axe."

Karston's eyes popped. "The Slits? The Slits? Let's get out of here!"

He raced over to flip the switch for the garage door, but with the power off, nothing happened. Idiot. Still, it was the right idea. Devin could grab the phone from the car and run to a neighbor's. He went up to the door and pulled. It rose an inch, but the bent slats wedged into the guide rail and the door stuck fast.

Oh crap.

The thrashing became more distant. Whoever it was seemed to be taking their time, maybe trying to do the most damage possible. Should he just bolt the door and wait it out until morning? But then they'd wreck his room, his things. His father's study, his mother's collection of Hummel figures. He and Cody had beaten them once before. He could do something. But what?

"I'll go get the phone in the kitchen," Devin said. "I'll have to be fast, before they come downstairs."

He was talking to himself, really, but Karston heard. "I'm not waiting for you alone in here! What if they get you?"

Karston was looking more frightened with each passing second. Devin wasn't doing much better; his heart was beating fast and his breathing was short and frantic.

"Okay, we'll both go in. I'll grab the phone," Devin said slowly, trying to catch his breath. "You open the sliding door off the dining room. Once I dial, we'll go out onto the deck and head for a neighbor's house. I won't even have to say anything; the police will come and they get here in like less than a minute."

"Really? Mrs. Wroth next door once called and it took two hours."

"Different neighborhood, Karston. Got it?"

"Got it."

His own hand shaking, Devin moved for the door, but Karston pulled him back.

"What if they come downstairs before I get to the door?"

Devin clenched his teeth. "Then hide. Just hide. And stay quiet."

"Where? Where should I hide?"

Devin whirled on him, furious. "Geez, man! There's a cupboard and two closets in there. I dunno! Fold yourself up and put yourself in the freaking toaster oven! Hide! This isn't like playing the bass, Karston! You've *got* to pull yourself together."

Karston nodded, but it was the same nod Karston had given him a hundred times that very night, right before he loused up the simplest bass line in the world. And here was Devin doing what he always told Cody not to, yelling at him, making him more nervous.

A sick feeling in Devin's stomach made him wonder if he might really die for this pathetic sack of self-consciousness. Whoever the Slits sent this time had to be worse, right? No. No, no, no. Everything would be fine. The sounds were still upstairs. The phone and the door weren't that far. He just needed Karston not to freak out.

He put his hand on Karston's shoulder and felt how badly he was shivering. He shook him, patted him, looked him in the eye. "We're going in now, okay? Just head for the door, slide it open, and run. That's all you have to do. You can do it."

Can't you?

All his pity for Karston vanished as he realized that in a situation like this—life or death—Karston could drag them both down.

Wasn't that what Cody was trying to say? Could that be Cody up there?

Swallowing, Devin walked up and felt the cold knob in his hand. He turned it and pulled the door open a crack, letting filtered street light into the sealed garage. He could see clearly enough, but all he had was a view of the small hallway that led to the kitchen, the door to the pantry closet, and the small room with the washer and dryer. The open door also gave him a different sense of the sounds. The banging was still violent, but more muffled, more clearly distant. The empty garage had acted like a big drum, amplifying the noise and making it echo.

Feeling like he could make it, Devin opened the door further. He stepped in, feeling Karston too close behind. If he stopped short, Karston would stumble right into him. So he didn't; he kept walking, out into the wide kitchen, past the beige Corian counters that looked yellow-gray in the night. He made for the phone that hung on the wall next to the far cabinet.

As he moved, he felt Karston still annoyingly close behind, so he waved him ahead, pointing toward the sliding door. Karston ambled on like he had all the time in the world, not moving nearly fast enough for Devin's taste. Devin got so wrapped up watching him, he nearly forgot to grab the phone when he reached it. As Karston finally made it to the sliding door, about ten yards from where Devin stood in the cavernous house, Devin grabbed the receiver, punched 911, and waited.

Almost instantly, there was squawking on the phone. An operator had picked up. Should he say something? If he had a whole conversation with them, he was afraid the Slits might hear. Sound traveled quickly through the air vents of the house. He could often hear his parents fighting down here, even when they spoke in what they thought were whispers. He thought about just dropping the receiver and going for the door, but wasn't sure. *Would* they come if he didn't speak? That's what his father had always said. He was usually right about that sort of thing.

"Come on!" Karston called, waving toward the open sliding door.

Great. Devin couldn't believe it. The idiot was still there, waiting for him at the door. Perfect.

Devin was about to keep the phone and run for the door when something rumbled, stumbled, and rolled down the main staircase. It sounded as if it had half leaped, then tripped down the carpeted stairs. Now it was scratching on the foyer's marble floor, clicking as if trying to get traction, like a dog making a turn on a slick, hard surface. What could be making such a weird noise? Had the Slit brought a pit bull with him? And carried it up the side of the garage and into the house? It didn't matter much. From the foyer, Devin knew, there was a perfect view of the dining room and the sliding door.

They must have heard Karston. That was it. They'd heard him, and now they were coming for him.

"Run!" Devin hissed.

"Come on!" Karston answered, still not running. Was he being stupidly loyal or just paralyzed with fear?

Out of the corner of his eye, Devin caught a moving shadow in the foyer. There was no way he'd make it to the sliding doors. But Karston could, he was standing right in front of them. And getting rid of Karston would triple his own chances of surviving.

"Don't wait! Just go!" was the last thing Devin said to Karston. Then, hoping he hadn't spoken too loudly, he raced back to the little hall in front of the garage door and hid in the pantry closet, pressing his back into the hard wire shelving to get the vented folding doors closed in front of him.

He figured Karston would be able to make it out the sliding door in time. He was, after all, only inches away. A turtle could do it. A turtle with bad legs. They might chase him out, but if Karston screamed for help, someone would hear him. And the police, the police would be here any minute.

But what if they didn't chase Karston? What if they headed for the garage? That was where they first tried to get in. Fortunately, the door had a dead bolt. When it was locked, you needed a key to get back in from the garage. If the Slits walked past Devin's hiding spot and entered, he could slam the door and lock them in. The door might give if they pounded it, but it would still slow them down enough for him to get out.

But that didn't happen. They didn't head for the garage. Instead, no sooner was Devin wincing from the spikes of the wires pressing into his back than he heard his band-mate call out, nice and loud, "Devin!"

Ack! Ack! Ack! Ack!

Shut up, Karston! Just shut up and run! For once in your life do the right thing!

"Devin! Help me!"

Devin furrowed his brow. He heard pain in the voice. A kind of craziness. Did the Slits have him? No.

Shut up! Just run! Save yourself and save me!

"Devin! He . . ."

There was a rush and a gasp. Something hit Karston. It sounded like it took him down. Devin was about to leap out, to try to help, but sirens filled the air. The police. The noise would drive the Slits off faster than he could. So he waited, counting the seconds, redeciding, until there came a weird guttural sound, like maybe that pit bull had been wounded. It was followed by a shredding, of cloth, or something thicker.

Karston started screaming. It wasn't even words, just raw air forced through tight vocal chords. Hearing the sheer agony in that voice, Devin spilled from the pantry closet and jumped into the shadowy kitchen.

The first thing he made out was a long smear of red along the white floor. It ran all thirty feet from the sliding doors into the kitchen. At the end of the kitchen, Karston was crumpled on the floor, looking more like a pile of laundry than a person, while something short and squat hovered in the darkness above him.

Devin's heart pounded. The sirens grew louder. Red and white lights flashed in from the window.

What the hell was that? A person?

A squarish head twitched on burly shoulders. Devin thought for a second he'd made eye contact, but decided that those couldn't be eyes.

It was too dark. Things were happening too quickly to be sure of anything. What came next had to be a trick of the light, an illusion caused by all the shadows and Devin's fear—it just had to—because as the figure stood and leaped over the Corian counter, Devin could swear its arms, which seemed hairy or wrapped in fur, were nearly twice as long as its short, stocky legs.

It bounded over the counter as if it were a fish

and the air were water. Its freakish shape sent expensive pots and pans flying. It hit the dining room floor amidst a clatter of metal and Teflon, then dove out the open sliding door that Karston had been too stupid or frightened to use himself.

Was it a dwarf? Some kind of bear? Devin was sweating, aside from being confused and frightened. He wondered if whatever it was hadn't been trying to trash the upstairs at all, but was just leaping around, an animal stuck in a too-small cage. Or a monster.

He snapped the elementary school fantasy from his head. It was some short, asshole body builder with a knife, that was all. He'd heard the sirens coming and jumped the counter for a faster escape.

Devin raced up to Karston and knelt beside him. He was cut up, badly. But what kind of knife could do something like this? His forearms jutted up at the elbows, but neither they nor his hands moved. His lower torso didn't move, either. The only part of him that did move was his head. It rocked back and forth, as if trying to pry itself away from the pain of his paralyzed body.

Shaking, Devin forced himself to move in closer.

The head steadied. Karston looked at him. "Sorry about stealing your money, Devin," he said weakly. His voice sounded wet and phlegmy, almost like he was gargling.

Devin scanned the body, torn between trying to do something about the bleeding and wondering if whatever he did might only make it worse. "Forget it. It's okay."

"You forgive me?"

"Yeah. Sure."

Not knowing what else he could do, Devin hesitated, but finally took Karston's hand and squeezed it. It felt cold. It didn't squeeze back.

"So, I'm still in the band?" Karston said.

The question caught Devin by surprise. Was it really *that* important to him? Or was he going into some kind of shock?

"Sure. You're still in the band," Devin said.

"I'm getting better, right? On the bass? It wasn't a waste, right?"

"Yeah, Karston. You're getting better. Really, man. Getting better every time," Devin said.

"Yeah?" Karston's voice was tired, distant. His eyes wavered, then steadied, focusing on something Devin couldn't see.

94

Blood pooled on the kitchen tile, running along the grout just like the drippings of the filet mignon.

Something sloshed beneath Karston's wet shirt. It may have just been more blood, or maybe he'd shifted in a funny way, but it looked as if pieces of Karston were tumbling out from beneath the cloth. Even if the ambulance came right now, right this second, Devin doubted it would make any difference.

"Yeah, Karston," Devin said. "You're the best. The best."

The funeral parlor was cheap and dark. A huge stain on the thin, crappy carpet gave off a moldy smell, and everywhere you walked, the floorboards creaked. Some of the bulbs in the lamps had blown, and the surface of the old paneling peeled in spots, revealing bits of straw-colored Masonite beneath.

But Karston—Karston looked even worse. His face was gray, and whoever had worked on the corpse had put eyeliner on him, badly, so he looked like some old-style glam rocker. The blue polyester suit he was stuffed into must have been worn last at his middle-school graduation, when he was two or three inches shorter.

It didn't matter to Karston, though. Karston was dead. If there was any kind of afterlife or whatever, Devin hoped it was at least a place where Karston wouldn't be afraid anymore. Or embarrassed. Or ashamed. Or picked on.

As he stood and stared at the body, Devin became aware that his own suit felt really hot, and the too-tight shirt neck was suffocating. If he puffed out his neck, he might be able to get the button to pop.

"Come on, you keep standing there like something's going to happen. Sit with me," Cheryl said, tugging at his arm. She looked funny in a black dress. It flattered her figure, but that seemed wrong under the circumstances. Her eyes were puffy from crying.

Devin nodded numbly. He let her lead him to the third row of folding seats, in front of his parents, where they sat down together.

As he settled, or tried to, Devin felt his father's hand on his shoulder, squeezing, patting. "Stay in your seat," his mother said, eyeing whoever came in. "Just stay down, Devin, please."

She'd been such a wreck after getting called back in the middle of her short vacation to learn that her home had been invaded, not only by some killer, but by scores of police. They'd grilled Devin for hours. He told them about the Slits, but nothing about how strange the attacker had looked in the shadow, except to say he was short, stout, and strong.

They said the damage in the house looked like standard vandalism, but it didn't look that way to Devin. A heavy end table had been splintered into firewood while a shelf of his mom's Hummel figures was left untouched. There was a shoulder-high crack in the plasterboard right next to a full-size mirror that hadn't been smashed. There were tears high up in the wall and even on the ceiling. But he supposed the police knew what they were doing.

After all, what was *standard* vandalism?

Still feeling hot and antsy, Devin looked around. Toward the back were a bunch of kids from Argus High School. Devin figured they didn't even know Karston, but were just here to gawk. Half were in street clothes, which Devin thought disrespectful, but at least they all wore the green armbands that had been given out in school in memoriam. He hadn't been back to Argus yet himself, but he knew that was all anyone was talking about. The story of the murder was the biggest thing to hit town in years.

"Look at the flowers my mother sent," he whispered to Cheryl. "They're huge and gaudy. Bigger than the ones from his mother. It's embarrassing."

Cheryl shrugged a little. "They're beautiful. But yeah, tacky. Aren't all the flowers tacky? Try to calm down."

"It's just . . . it's just . . . I guess seeing him again made me realize he's dead," Devin said. "I'd sort of forgotten that part."

"Yeah," Cheryl said. She took his hand and patted it, trying to make him feel better. But he didn't. Even her hand felt uncomfortable. "It's not your fault, you know."

Isn't it? Are you sure? If I had jumped out when he called me the first time, instead of waiting, Karston might still be alive.

He looked around again. Seeing Torn's keyboard player a few rows back, Devin managed a weak wave of his fingers.

"There's One Word Ben," Devin whispered to Cheryl. "But where the hell is Cody? He should be here."

"His little brother has a fever. They had to find a sitter," Cheryl said.

Devin was about to ask how she happened to know that when, with a loud creak of floorboard, Cody stepped in, looking totally surreal. He had on a dark suit and black T-shirt, but no tie. His savage white hair was actually de-spiked and combed into a part, like he was some lame gangster wannabe.

He cracked his neck, then walked up to Karston's mom, leaned forward, and whispered to her.

At least he's being respectful.

She didn't seem to be paying much attention to whatever Cody was saying. She looked drugged or drunk, but maybe it was grief. Cody straightened and motioned for Devin to join him at the casket.

He felt a pull from Cheryl's hands and heard an exasperated whisper from his mother, but ignored both and went back up to the casket for what was probably the tenth time. After Cody crossed himself, they stood side by side, facing the body.

"Check out my hair," Cody whispered. "You believe what my stepmother made me do to it?"

Devin looked over his shoulder and saw Cody's

100

parents walk in with a few of his brothers and sisters. His father was tall and broad. He'd been some kind of athlete years back and even now had no paunch. His stepmother had insanely curly hair and a few of the kids had a familiar wild glint in their eyes. Despite the glint, Devin had always been disappointed by how normal they all seemed compared to Cody.

"Your hair looks like crap," Devin said stiffly. "Is that what you want to talk about?"

Cody looked at him a second, then shook his head, deciding to let it go. "Nah. Got good news for you. You know our two friends, Nick and Jake from the Slits?"

"Yeah?"

"My dad just got the call. They arrested them with like two sacks of crystal meth. Even if they can't pin the murder on them, they're gone, man, gone for a long, long time. Rumor is they're ratting out their brothers for reduced sentences, so even the rest of the Slits won't care what happens to them."

Cody slapped Devin in the shoulder and grinned. "We're clear, man, free and clear!"

Devin should have felt relieved, but he didn't.

Instead he said, "Shh! It's Karston's funeral! Keep it down."

Cody made another face, then forced a more somber expression to his features. They both stood there awhile, looking at the dead boy. After it started to feel too long, Cody said, "Well, you know, this does kind of solve our other problem. Now you don't have to fire him."

Devin flushed with anger. Words forced their way out as he desperately tried to keep his voice low in the funeral parlor. "How can you be such an ass?"

The last word was loud enough to earn a "Shh!" from someone in the front row.

Cody pulled him away from the casket. Devin shook his arm free and kept walking, out into the quiet lobby where the moldy smell was only slightly dampened, then through the glass doors and out onto the sidewalk, where the sky was dark, the wind cool, and cars rolled by, going about their business as if no one had died at all.

Cody popped out of the door behind him. He came up, pulled out a pack of cigarettes, and shook one out toward Devin. There was a time when Devin had pretended he smoked, to impress people like Cody, but that time had passed. He shook his head no.

Cody popped one in his mouth, lit, and took a drag. "Look, Devin, I'm not saying it's a *good* thing. I didn't not like Karston or anything. I wouldn't wish that on people I hated. Man, his face looks like putty. But we're here now, and sooner or later, here is where we're going to have to move on from."

"Yeah, well, you ever stop to think that if maybe you hadn't borrowed money you couldn't pay back that we might *not* be here? That Karston might be alive? Or if I hadn't helped you that *you'd* be dead now instead of him?" Devin said.

Cody took a step back. "Whoa. Now *that's* cold."

A few Argus kids stepped out from the funeral parlor. One was listening to something. Seeing Cody and Devin, he stopped and gave them the thumbs-up.

"Torn rocks!" he said. He pulled out an earbud and held it toward them. Even with the tiny volume, Devin recognized a few beats from "Face," the MP3 they'd finally made with his bass line. Devin told Cody it was Karston on bass, and Cody didn't bother to question it, maybe because the rumor that the "dead kid" was playing on it gave the cut some steam.

"All right!" Cody said, grinning back and playing some air guitar.

A girl in the group wearing a red hooded sweatshirt said, "When are we going to hear the haunted song?"

"The what?" Devin said, scrunching his face.

The girl shrugged. "That song you were playing the night he died."

"How did you . . . ?" Devin started, but Cody cut him off.

"Soon! Soon!" he said. Then he slapped Devin on the shoulder and said, "Hey, I forgot to mention, I fixed your song."

"*Fixed?*"

"Here's a preview!" he said to the group. Playing his best air guitar, he screeched:

I'm lyin' to the angels,
Lyin' to the angels . . .

Devin shoved him. "Stop it! We're in front of a funeral parlor!" When Cody didn't respond immediately, Devin shoved him again, harder.

"Oh yeah, right. He's right, you know. Catch you later!"

Smiling and nodding, the group wandered off.

Devin glared at Cody.

Cody made his face sheepish and sad. "You're right. That was wrong. That was really wrong."

"The haunted song?"

"I had nothing to do with that. Nothing. It's a chat room thing. I don't know where they got it," Cody said, but he looked like he was lying. He tossed his cigarette down and stomped on it. "But why not take advantage of it? It's like the Blair Witch."

Before Devin could quit Torn in disgust, One Word Ben and Cheryl emerged from the funeral parlor. Cody nodded at Ben. "You still in? You can pick up the bass."

Ben nodded. "Yeah."

"All right!" Cody shouted, again too loud.

"In? In with what?" Devin asked.

Cody smiled. "We've been invited back to Tunnel Vision. A whole night's ours if we want, for a tribute to Karston. We're going to need at least twenty minutes to do a full set."

"And when were you going to mention that to me?" Devin asked.

Cody shrugged. "I was like, trying to respect your grieving process. I've been waiting for you to bring up Torn, man. But you didn't."

"It's cold," Cheryl said as she slid next to Devin and shivered. He opened his jacket and wrapped it half around her, but he kept staring at Cody.

"What else has been going on without me, Cody? If you didn't tell them about the song, how could they know about it? There isn't even a recording."

He felt Cheryl stiffen. There was something strange about the way she and Cody looked at each other.

"Yeah, there is," she said quietly.

Devin stared at her. "*You* started that rumor?"

She shrugged. "All my friends heard the story and everyone kept nagging me. So I told them what you saw in the shadows and all. And I put the video on our site. . . ."

Devin's brow furrowed. "The one you took of me singing the song."

For the second time, Devin was about to quit in frustration, when a creaking voice like a dying animal called to them from the door.

"Get out of here!" it said. "How dare you stand

106

around like a street gang in front of my son's funeral! You don't have any damn respect! Nothing!"

Karston's mother staggered toward them. As Devin had thought, she was drunk. She wore an ill-fitting black dress, and the edges of the shawl wrapped around her shoulders lifted in the breeze. Strange, but he'd never seen her standing before. Even in the funeral parlor, she never got up. Now he could clearly see how short she was, and that there was something wrong with her back that made her wrinkled face lean forward from a curved neck. As she walked, it looked like her angry, accusing face was coming closer all on its own, without her body.

"You make me sick. Thieves and a slut! You're all worthless!" she shouted. "That should be you in there, all of you, not him! He never hurt nobody in his life, nobody! And he idolized you! He was too stupid to see what you really were."

They were all silent, terrified, ashamed. Even Cody.

We're sorry! Devin was about to say, but the words never made it out.

"You killed him!" she shouted. "Killed my boy."

She lurched forward and swatted Cody in the shoulder. Maybe it was because he happened to be closest, maybe because his white hair color made him easier to see. He moved his hands to block further blows, but none came. Instead, she sneered, spun, walked across the street, and entered a bar.

The four of them watched her go, staying silent until the wooden, windowless door of the bar swung closed.

Cody nudged Devin. "Hey, why don't you go in there now and offer to buy the bass?"

He started laughing. It was so stupid and ridiculous, Ben started laughing too. Even Cheryl snickered before she stopped herself.

"I don't believe you," Devin said, shaking his head. "I don't believe any of you."

He pulled back, swung, and punched Cody full in the mouth. Cody stopped laughing and staggered back.

"Hey!" he snarled. He wiped his mouth and looked at the blood on his fingers. "Hey!" he said even louder. He tensed, pulled back, ready to swing.

Devin just stood there, as if saying, *Go ahead, do it.*

But he'd helped Cody against the Slits. And Cody needed him for the band.

Cody dropped his fist, then wiped his mouth again.

Cheryl leaped between them. "There was something weird on the videotape," she said. "That's what started the rumor."

"Something weird?" Devin said, exhaling to calm himself. *Is she using bright and shiny objects to distract me now, too?*

"I've been wanting to show it to you, but you seemed so out of it, the timing didn't feel right. I've got it here," she said. She stepped a few cars down to her parents' white Lexus, popped the trunk, and pulled out her camcorder. All four gathered around the tiny color LCD viewscreen. Devin and Cody sneered at each other when they accidentally touched.

The picture was easy enough to see. There was Devin on his stool, picking at the strings of the Ovation. Karston was leaning against the wall behind him. At first it didn't seem like anything was strange, but then he noticed some tiny, swirling spots, first near the guitar's fretboard, then near his mouth, then around his head, and

Karston's, too. They were small. Unless you were looking for something, you'd never see them.

"See?" Cheryl said.

"Isn't that cool?" Cody said, grinning again.

But One Word Ben shook his head and said, "Dust."

Devin nodded. "Yeah, I saw it on one of those *Ghost Hunters* shows. Dust gets in the lens and a bunch of loser geeks think it's spirit orbs or something."

Cody turned to him, annoyed. "Don't ruin it! Don't tell anyone that! This is great for us! We can play the song at Tunnel Vision!"

Cheryl looked at Devin, waiting for his judgment.

Devin shrugged. "But it's dust."

Just dust. As in ashes to ashes, dust to dust.

Only this dust swirled, spun, and seemed to dance in tune to the music.

Big and brown, the featureless walls and huge windows covered with protective metal grids made Argus High School look more like a three-story factory than it did an educational institute. It had one of the lowest percentages of graduates who went on to college in the state, and an even lower percentage of students who graduated, period. It was shaped, appropriately enough, like a big *L*.

The first thing Devin noticed upon his return to its hallowed halls were posters on the walls.

Though Devin had never officially said he wanted back in the band, he'd never said no, either. A strange enthusiasm about the ghost song and the big club date had taken over his band-mates, even Cheryl, so he, as usual, had shut up and gone along

TORN

Friday, May 23, 9 p.m.
at Tunnel Vision
Hear the song that's haunting the net
"Lying to the Angels"
LIVE!

For Karston
Bring your soul. If you don't use it, don't be afraid to lose it.

for the ride. It wasn't so bad, he realized now. The posters were pretty cool—respectful but edgy. The art he recognized as Cheryl's, but it seemed like some of the phrasing had to be Cody's. And maybe it *would* be for Karston, in a way.

The second thing he noticed as he walked down the crowded halls toward homeroom was that people were stopping their conversations to gawk at him. They weren't pitying looks, exactly. There was something else in their eyes: a respectful curiosity. The stares were familiar, but Devin couldn't quite place them until he realized they were the same kind of looks he'd gotten when he'd left the stage at Tunnel Vision. It felt . . . good, but he didn't quite want it to.

Fear of another attack from the Slits was a vague tingle at best. After the meth bust, Nick and Jake turned state witness, which led to ten more arrests. There were still no charges for the murder, though. Devin had been asked to look at a lineup, and while one short muscular hood had looked hauntingly familiar, he couldn't quite square him with what he'd seen leaping about his kitchen. He gave the police a maybe, but in his own mind, Devin was now convinced the shadows had played tricks on him. A Slit had killed Karston. It had to be.

In any case, the gang had been effectively gutted both by the police and a storm of publicity. Their colors hadn't been seen on the streets in days. Devin knew that it wasn't because Karston had been killed; it was because Karston had been killed in Meadowcrest Farms. Knowing that made him sick.

Down the hall, by the entrance to the gym, he spotted Cheryl, wearing cute green shorts and a T-shirt. She was using an open stapler to put up more posters. Happy to see her, he sped up, about to call her name, when he suddenly felt a tap on his shoulder.

He turned to see a few guys and some girls staring at him. One of the boys, a gangly sort with long hair, a faded jacket, and a noticeable slump, nodded at Devin, then toward one of the posters on the wall.

"You're in that band? You're in Torn?" he said with a bit of a slur.

Devin nodded. They all smiled slightly and nodded back in tandem, saying things like "Cool" and "All right." The wave of approval from people he didn't know at all was strong and strange. Devin started to feel really good about it in spite of his reservations. In fact, it was probably the first time he'd felt good since Karston died.

What should he say to them? Cody was good at this kind of thing, but he was home these days. "So, you coming to the show?" he asked, hoping it didn't sound too lame.

The nodding became more enthusiastic.

"Yeah."

"You bet."

"You guys rock."

Well, that was easy.

He tried to keep cool, but a small smile curled his lips. Before he could say anything else though, another hand found his shoulder and gently pulled him around.

"See?" Cheryl said. "You're famous now."

"Right," Devin said.

"No. Enjoy it," she said. She kissed him. "But don't forget the rest of us mortals."

With that, she wandered off down the halls, the tops and bottoms of the posters in her hand rising and falling as she went, earning her own respect-ful stares.

Devin turned back to his small group, his smile now full blown.

"And did you write that song on the site? About the angels?"

"Yeah, it's mine."

Except for that chorus Cody added . . .

"And you're gonna sing it at the show?"

"That's the idea. Well, Cody will sing it."

"The guy who got kicked out. Yeah, that's what I meant." But then the gangly kid took a nervous step closer and whispered, "So are all the rumors true, man?"

You mean about the ghosts on the video? I'll have to be careful about that one—Cody wants our "legend" to build. Maybe it's not such a bad idea.

"What rumors do you mean?" Devin said, trying to seem innocent.

"You know," the kid said with a knowing smirk. "That you killed that loser Karston just to get his bass."

That afternoon, Devin and Cheryl sat at "their" place, a huge rock just outside town, watching white clouds roll and billow in the blue sky. The rock was atop a low hill that sat at the edge of an abandoned development. Construction had stopped due to bankruptcy. The roads there were dirt, leading to various holes in the ground that had been dug out by backhoes for concrete foundations that were never poured, and then left to collapse or fill with rainwater. At their backs, new McMansion rooftops peeked through thinner woods that sat along the dirt road, but ahead of them, the forest began.

Cheryl tried to comfort him, hugging him steadily. "It's just a stupid rumor," she said.

"Yeah? Later in the day some other kids said they heard we'd sacrificed Karston to a demon in exchange for a killer song. It's all just too weird."

"There've been so many hits on the site, the server crashed again," she said, nudging him.

"It's not because the song's any good—it's because Karston died," Devin answered. "Is this how you want to make it big?"

"But the song *is* good. It's great. The rest is just an accident. You've got to believe in it, Devin. I do."

He said nothing.

Finally, she shrugged. "Maybe you should think about something else. At least the police unsealed the crime scene and let you back into your house."

Devin wanted to laugh at the irony. "We were better off at the hotel. Mom swears she can still see Karston's blood on the kitchen tiles, and she's got enough tranquilizers in her to stop a bull elephant. It's like a freaking scene from *Macbeth*. I try to convince her it's just the stains from the filet mignon that we ... that I ..." Devin paused. "Christ, Cheryl, it could've been you."

She pulled him close again. "No. You would have protected me."

Would he? Would he have done any better a job if it had been Cheryl?

"How's your dad?"

"He's been great, attentive, supportive. Even took time from work just to be with us. I didn't know he had it in him. And then last night, he even told me I shouldn't give up on the band because of ..."

Instead of finishing his sentence, Devin stared off. Nothing had been normal since the killing. His time with Cheryl now was supposed to be a normal thing, and it wasn't turning out normal at all.

"So what'd you tell him?" Cheryl asked. He'd nearly forgotten she was there.

"About what?"

"Torn. You've never actually said you want the group to go on. Do you?"

"I don't know. I don't even want to decide."

Nothing new about that, though, is there?

He looked at her, her skin shining in the sun, face placid.

"What about you?" he asked. "What do you want? Even with all these sick rumors, do you really think we should still have the band?"

She looked at him a moment, as if the answer should be obvious. He'd always suspected, hoped really, that she'd just joined to be with him, but they'd never actually talked about it. If that was it, here was her chance to get out. And maybe his, too. Maybe they could go to law school together.

"Well . . . isn't that really the kind of thing you have to decide for yourself?" she said slowly.

"Yeah, I guess, but . . . I just need to think about it," he said. "How are your parents dealing?" he asked, changing the subject.

She stood up on the uneven rock and stretched her lean form. Devin watched it against the white and blue. He wanted to grab her, but figured it wouldn't be right, like they should still be in mourning or something.

"They're upset, but they'll get over it. I'm there if you need me," she said. "But we should probably start rehearsing soon if we're going to do anything."

If you need me. Maybe she *was* only in Torn to be with him.

Wouldn't that be something?

"Did you hear?" Cheryl asked.

"Now what?"

"Cody got Karston's bass. He talked Allen Bates into being our manager and Mr. Bates bought it from Karston's mom," she explained.

Sure, Devin thought. Why not? Another icon added to the growing local legend. Haunted song. Haunted bass. Haunted band.

When the time finally came, Tunnel Vision was
packed. It wasn't just full. It wasn't just standing
room only. It was packed. From his view behind
the stage's brand-new curtain, Devin could see all
the way to the twin exits at the back of the tunnel.
Even so, all he could make out of the mob was a
sea of arms, torsos, and heads pushed together so
tightly he couldn't figure out which appendage
belonged to which body. He did catch flashes of
blue uniforms and caps.

"The police are here, too," Devin said. They'd
seen three squad cars parked outside when they
arrived. That was most, if not all, of the city's small
force.

"Yeah." He heard Cody chortle behind him. "We've got a *police* presence, because Torn is too freaking cool."

Devin shook his head. "It's not because Torn is all that, Cody. It's the murder. Remember, we're only famous because Karston died."

"Now, maybe," Cody said. "But soon it's gonna be the music."

Cheryl sat behind her drum kit. She stretched up her long arms, folded them behind her head, and bent forward, getting her muscles ready for the gig. "Bates said we're way over the safety limit, and they're spilling out into the parking lot," she said. "They're afraid of a riot."

Devin's mind went to a story his mother kept telling him about a fire in a rock club years ago where ninety-six people died.

Cody eyed him. "Terrified or jazzed?"

Devin thought about it a second. He was still furious at Cody for his behavior at the funeral parlor, but if they were going to play together, he might as well talk to the guy. "Both," he said.

Cody blew some air between his lips. "Fence hugger." He twisted his head toward the others. "You guys?"

Cheryl also said, "Both." There seemed something strange in the way she looked at Cody.

One Word Ben, strapping on Karston's bass, nodded his agreement. "Both."

Cody chuckled. "Well, I guess we are really Torn, then."

Do you ever shut up, Cody?

"Two minutes," someone shouted.

Devin moved back from the curtain and sat on the stool they'd brought from the garage. That was Cody's idea, too. He figured people would recognize it from the video. Half the crowd out there had video cameras, hoping to catch the little orbs when they played. The other half had probably shown up to see the kids they thought were killers.

The whole thing made Devin queasy: the fact that the show was advertised as a memorial, the fact that it would be the first time they played "Lying to the Angels" live. The question remained: Was this really how he wanted to become famous?

But he knew, in the end, as Cheryl had hinted and Cody had said, all the accidental notoriety could only provide a boost. In the end it would be the song. His song. Well, his and Cody's, now that the so-called chorus had been worked in.

Freaking Cody, fixing his song.

And, technically, it was his and Cody's and his grandmother's. Devin caught an image of Namana sitting by his bedside, stroking his head as she sang, warning him to be good, be good, be good, with a stuffed toy lying beside him on the pillow. As he lifted the Ovation, now fitted with pickups, he eyed Cody, wondering if his anger showed. "Respectful, right?"

Cody made his face somber to the extreme. "You know it."

Cody strode to his spot behind the central mike, stretched, and yawned like a carefree dog; then he stood straight, looking . . . respectful.

How does he do that? Devin wondered. *Does he not feel? Is part of his brain just missing?*

A rush of sound enveloped them. Devin saw the curtain rope scrape against the pulley, but couldn't hear it. The applause was too loud. The thick cloth rose and there they were, exposed to wave upon wave of approval.

They ripped through a few songs: "Face," "If It Doesn't Kill You," and the cover of "Hey Bulldog" that Cody had been dying to play. With One Word

Ben on bass they were tighter than ever, and they had more than enough numbers for a full twenty-minute set.

Playing without Karston was like having lead weights removed from his hands and head, a feeling that made Devin feel sick and even angrier at Cody for being right.

Through it all, through every song, the crowd kept chanting, " 'Lying to the Angels,' 'Lying to the Angels'!"

They were planning to do another few numbers first, but the chanting had grown too loud. Finally, Cody put his head down theatrically, then raised a single finger to quiet the crowd. After a moment, it actually worked. When the sound dropped enough, he spoke softly, somberly, into the mike, saying only, "For Karston."

The space was flooded with sound: a torrent of slamming hands mixed with wild shrieks. It got so loud, the cops in back shifted nervously. All the while, Cody just stood there, the picture of sadness, holding his head down, letting the tip of his white hair touch the mike. Cheryl and Ben were like zombies, expressionless. Devin figured he looked the same, but also knew their dull shock would be mistaken for something deeper, like mourning.

They all waited for the new round of applause to die down. Devin had no real sense of time, but he'd have sworn it went on for five minutes. And what were they cheering for? Not Karston, whom none of them had really known. Was it all just for the creepy haunted song? Was it for death in general?

Some in the crowd finally realized Torn wasn't going to play until they stopped, so loud shushing mixed with the roar. As the shushing rose, the roar quieted. For a second, only the shushing was left, like a host of strange hissing insects. Then it, too, faded.

The whole crowd, the whole huge crowd crammed into the converted train tunnel, fell completely, totally silent.

Cody gave a nearly imperceptible nod of his head. Cheryl clicked her sticks four times. Devin started finger picking.

It was the most complicated thing he'd ever played in public. It started on an E minor. On the second measure, Ben came in on Karston's bass.

As Devin stayed on the E minor, Ben walked

down to D-sharp, D, C-sharp. Together, they hit a C and a G, right on time. *Funny,* Devin thought, *we could never play this song "for Karston" if Karston were playing.* Cody came in with his raspy, deep voice:

> *Sun is low, the sky gray, gray, gray,*
> *All day's colors gone,*
> *Your heart beats slowly, drowsy eyes,*
> *Soon your dreams will come.*

It was amazing. It wasn't quite the melody as Devin had written it—Cody was improvising as usual—but it was low and mournful, and the wildness in Cody's voice sounded like it was being held back by thick chains of sadness.

Devin joined in on the verses. He was sort of a control track for Cody's total improv, reminding himself how the song had actually been written.

After the second verse, Cheryl slammed out a hard steady beat and Cody went wild with his shrieking chorus:

> *So now I'm lying to angels,*
> *Lying to the angels, baby ...*

If the crowd had been excited before, now it went insane, hooting, hollering, and throbbing as if everyone had been twisted together into one giant, monster thing. Devin couldn't hear himself play or sing. He had no idea if he was on tempo, but it really didn't matter. The moment had blown past the song.

This was usually where Devin would pull back into himself, watch himself watch himself, but not this time. Whatever had grabbed the crowd grabbed Devin, too, mixing with his anger at, and awe for, Cody. He played hard, frantically. It felt as if all his frustration, fear, and rage were flooding out his fingertips and his throat, out into the speakers and the world, calling out into the void, hoping something would answer, but not knowing, or caring, what it would be.

So lay your head down, rest, rest, rest,
And when the angels ask,
Tell them just how good you've been
As long as the darkness lasts.

When Torn finished "Lying to the Angels," the crowd started roaring again. Devin thought it was a more subdued, thoughtful sound, as if the song had moved them, but then realized they might just be tired of cheering.

What he didn't kid himself about was the slew of foul language that came from somewhere in the back. Scanning for the source, he thought he saw some fists and arms flying. In seconds, a swarm of blue swept toward the spot, shoving people out of the way and into one another as it went.

Cody saw it, too. "Be cool, people," he said into the mike, but the only effect of his announcement was that the people jammed in front now tried to turn around to see what was going on. Near the stage they were so tightly packed, some couldn't even manage that. For the moment, their frustration expressed itself as a pained wriggling, but Devin feared it could quickly turn ugly.

The angry shouts continued, with more voices joining. The police, frustrated at being unable to get through, grabbed some of the people in the crowd. The people, probably not even realizing who was grabbing them, fought back. More fists flew.

The group up front looked ready to panic. It seemed everyone was.

"Wow, this is turning into a riot," Cody said.

"Let's play," Devin said, hoping a song would distract at least most of the crowd. Cody, who actually looked a little frightened himself for a change, nodded. Devin turned up his volume and slammed the first chord of "Chili Bone Finger" on the Ovation. Nothing came out. The power to their amps had been cut.

As the shouting grew louder, Devin looked around the stage, perplexed. He saw Allen Bates frantically waving them toward the back room. One Word Ben was already unplugged and heading offstage, Cheryl following. Cody looked at Devin, shrugged, unplugged his guitar, and walked off. Devin couldn't do anything but follow.

The sounds behind them grew louder and more chaotic. Bates raised his voice. "It's a mess. We're being shut down. They've got more squad cars coming. Don't worry, everyone will be all right, but I want you guys out of here. Come on."

Devin and Ben laid down their guitars, but Cody refused to let go of his Les Paul as they followed Bates through the back. He pointed down a flight of stone steps that led into a small dank tunnel.

"You want us to go down there?" Devin said. *Alone?*

"Where's it go?" Cheryl asked.

"It's an access tunnel to the children's furniture store, built back when it used to be a warehouse," Bates said. He was in a hurry, casting nervous glances back over his shoulder as his cell phone vibrated and chimed. He grimly ignored it, fished out a key, and handed it to Devin.

"Your folks dropped you off with your equipment, right?"

Devin nodded. It had been meant as a big show of support. They were all supposed to go out for steak dinner afterward, a treat from his father.

"I'll make sure they get out of the club and I'll have them pick you up in the parking lot out in back of the store," Bates said. "Until they show up, pretend you're the Beatles and try not to be seen." The phone chirped and buzzed again. Bates looked back and forth nervously. "You'll be fine. No one knows about the tunnel. I've got to get back before they destroy the place."

He whirled, but before he could leave, Cody called to him. "So, Allen! Still want us back next week?"

Bates gave him a weird grin. "Ha. Yeah. If I can afford the insurance." Then he vanished toward the noise, flipping open his phone as he went.

As a group, they shrugged and walked down the steps. The air felt cold after the heat of the lights and the crowd. The sounds, now above them, seemed far away. After using the key on a big green fire door, they climbed another set of steps and emerged into the quiet furniture store on its main floor, facing the display windows.

The scene was surreal. All around them were cribs, bassinets, and mock children's bedrooms. Red and blue lights flashed through the windows, casting strange shadows and giving the walls eerie, alternating colors. Looking outside, they again saw the three police cars at the front entrance to Tunnel Vision. Quite a presence for the small local force, but Devin guessed they were probably curious about the song, too.

Then again, it was way too few police to handle the crowd that was already on the street. It looked like it was the mess Bates had described—People were flooding out, walking in the middle of the avenue. They looked dazed and tired, but at least they were leaving and no one seemed hurt.

Devin didn't know what to think. Cheryl was clearly upset. One Word Ben looked ashen.

Cody was ecstatic.

"This is great! Amazing! We'll hit all the local papers. Maybe the story will even go national. We could have a record contract by the end of the week!"

"And if people die in a stampede?" Devin said in disgust as he flipped open his cell. "Don't you ever quit?"

Cody's Les Paul, still strapped to him, wobbled as he pivoted toward Devin. "Will you cut it out? Can't you just enjoy something for a change?"

"Which part am I supposed to enjoy? The riot? The fight with the Slits? Karston's murder at my house? You know, some of those people think *I* killed Karston."

There was an anger in his voice that threatened to rise into rage.

Cody shrugged. "Well, our fight with the Slits was pretty cool, wasn't it? You felt good after that, didn't you? It's like your ass is always half empty!"

"Do you mean my glass?"

"Whatever."

Devin exhaled and punched "1" on his speed

dial, trying to crush the phone with his thumb as if it were Cody's face. Bates was on the case, but their parents had all agreed to sit together at the show, and Devin promised to call if there were any change in plans. This counted as a change in plans.

His mother's pained voice filled the speaker, rising above the shouts behind her. "Where are you? Are you all right? Everyone's worried sick!"

Devin imagined his band-mates could hear every word.

"We're fine, Mom. Mr. Bates took us to the furniture store next door. You all okay?"

"Oh, thank God!" she said. "We're good. We're still inside. The police are taking everyone out in groups. They're very distracted. It doesn't look as if they've handled this sort of thing before and there doesn't seem to be enough of them. We have to talk about this. I don't know if I want you leading this kind of life."

Devin rolled his eyes. "Signal's breaking up, Mom. Can't really hear you. Pick us up in the parking lot in back of the store."

"Honey, our car may be blocked. Sit tight and we'll be there just as soon as we can."

"Okay." Devin snapped the phone closed and looked at the others. "It might be a while."

"Told you we should have driven ourselves," Cody said.

"What do you mean *we*? When did you get a car?" Devin shot back.

"Whatever."

One Word Ben moved toward a wall switch. "Lights?"

"No!" Cheryl said. "The crowd will see us. It might start more trouble."

For the first time, Devin noticed she was shaking. He came up and gave her a hug. "This is all pretty freaky, huh?" she said.

"We'll get past it," Devin said. He pressed his lips against her forehead.

She stiffened. Cody seemed annoyed by the display of affection.

What's that about?

"I'm going to go take a leak," Cody said.

He started walking toward the rear of the huge store, shifting his guitar so it was slung over his back.

"Just make sure you use the bathroom," Devin called after him.

135

"Ha ha," Cody answered, his voice already seeming far off.

One Word Ben wandered among the cribs, idly swatting the stuffed moons and teddy bears dangling from the mobiles. Their long shadows swirled across the room, forming bizarre twisted shapes on the walls and ceiling.

Devin turned back to Cheryl, feeling bad about how scared she seemed. Torn. It was all Torn's fault. Maybe she was realizing that now; maybe she'd finally had enough of Torn.

"We can quit, you know," he said softly. "We'd still be together, even without the group."

She furrowed her brow at him like he was crazy. "No," she said. "I don't want to quit. I've been practicing drums for years. Ever since I was a little girl I've wanted to be famous and play in a band. This is my dream."

Her words felt like a cold glass of water dumped on his head. All at once he realized Cheryl's commitment was never just to him; it was to herself, to her drumming. He felt like a total ass.

She looked at him, confused, as if she were seeing him for the first time, too. "I thought it was yours, too. I thought that was something we shared. You do want it, don't you? I mean, you're so talented. You couldn't just want to throw that away, could you?"

It was the conversation with Cody all over again. He shrugged, feeling himself on the fence yet again. "Yeah, I guess, but . . ."

A loud scraping from above echoed through the large open space, making all three heads turn upward toward the darkness. Unlike the muffled shouts and movement on the street outside, this sounded closer, more intimate.

Familiar.

It skittered across the width of the roof, seemed to stumble into a metal vent, then moved steadily, rapidly toward the back.

"Let's go wait in the parking lot," Devin said. "Now."

He started pulling Cheryl toward the side door. One Word Ben was way ahead of them.

Cheryl resisted. "What about Cody?" she said, worried.

He wanted to say, *What about him?*, but instead he called out across the quiet space. "Cody! Let's get going!"

A muffled slamming sound rumbled through the darkness. It could have been the door of a bathroom stall closing. Then there was nothing.

Oh, damn.

"Later," One Word Ben said as he vanished through the door.

Devin's heart thudded its way into his throat. Could it still be the Slits? Cornering them for a final vengeance?

"Cody?" he called, louder.

The slamming came again, followed by a series of thuds. Devin walked toward the middle of the display room, Cheryl beside him.

"Go wait outside," he told her.

"No," she said, annoyed.

Past long rows of brightly colored bureaus and changing tables, he saw the gray men's room door. It was slamming against its frame, rattling as if a fight were going on behind it.

"Cody!" he cried.

A sound came out, low and rough. It could've been Cody calling for help, or it could've been something else entirely. Devin quickened his pace, Cheryl behind him.

There was a chemical fire extinguisher and an axe behind a glass door on the wall between the two restrooms. Devin grabbed the extinguisher. He was surprised to see Cheryl grab the axe.

"No," he said. "Call the cops. They're right out-side."

She nodded and grabbed her cell.

The door was still slamming. Inhaling, Devin held out the spray end of the extinguisher and kicked the door in.

It was pitch-black in the windowless room. Short shadows twisted on the floor. Fearful he might spray Cody in the face by mistake, and not knowing what else to do, Devin flipped on the lights.

Shredded ceiling tiles made him glance up at a torn hole that seemed carved out of the building. Then he saw Cody on the floor, pulling at the tiles with his hands, trying to crawl to the door. His long fingers scrabbled among little sharp pieces of something scattered on the floor. They were sharp, wooden, but some were shiny and colored. It was like Cody's Les Paul, shattered.

What could have happened to it? What was going on?

Unlike the attack at home in the dark, here the fluorescents gave Devin a perfect view of the thing Cody was trying to get away from. And his world came apart.

At first glance it seemed a formless mass of black fur, giving the impression of a deformed bear. But on closer inspection, as its vile features became clearer, it didn't look anything like a bear. It had a leathery nose like a bat's and a flat squat face that looked like dark, greasy rubber. Its wide round mouth held both viper fangs and pointy rows of teeth. Maybe three feet tall, it crouched on thick legs that were so short they may as well have been stumps—stumps that ended not in feet or paws, but in leathery hooves. At the end of its hairy arms, which were twice as long as its body, it had sharp bony claws.

Those arms were wrapped around Cody's legs like snakes, as if they had four or five joints in them instead of the usual elbow and wrist. Those claws were up near his abdomen, their points prodding, trying to slip beneath his shirt, to his skin.

And none of that was the most horrible thing. The most horrible thing was that Devin couldn't shake the feeling he'd seen this impossible creature somewhere before. Yes, he'd seen it back at his house, in the shadows, when it attacked Karston, but it was more than that, an older memory, as if he'd somehow known this grotesque thing all his life. As if his own brain were saying, *Of course, this is it!*

The sudden light surprised the fiend. The yellow of its eyes smoked over into black and it reared in annoyance. Feeling his legs briefly free, Cody kicked the monster in the chest. Its long arms loosened further, letting a frenetic Cody slip from its pythonlike grasp. In less than a second, he was half on his feet, scrambling, screaming, and bolting past Devin, out the door and into the store beyond.

Before Devin's log-jammed brain could even register what was going on, he was alone with it in the bathroom.

It raised its head. The original squash-yellow of its eyes returned and the orbs seemed to focus on Devin. Its mouth opened into a perfect circle and it growled. The sound that came from it was more like a wind than anything animal or human.

Where have I seen this before?

Before he could wonder further, Devin's instincts took over. He raised the extinguisher and pressed the lever, sending a long thick stream of white foam out across the bathroom and into the rubbery, batlike face.

Eyes blacking over again, the thing reeled at the chemical assault. Its arms curled and the claws curved backward to wipe the stinging foam away from its face, but by then, Devin had hurled the metal canister at it and was out the door himself.

Bursting out, he nearly rammed into Cheryl. She was standing by the door. From the twisted look of terror on her face, she'd obviously caught a glimpse inside.

"What is it? What is it?" she shrieked. Devin was too busy shoving her toward the exit to answer. He reached the door that led to the rear of the building and flung it open, pulling them both out into the cool night air. He didn't stop to look back until they were halfway across the huge parking lot. It didn't seem to be following.

Then, gasping for breath, he said, "Did you call the cops? Did you tell them?"

She nodded. "The dispatcher said they were having trouble with their radios, but she'd send someone as soon as she could."

Okay then, they could all just walk to the front of the store together. He looked around. One Word Ben was sitting on a steel post near a streetlight at the far end of the lot, as far away as he could possibly get and still see his parents when they came. When he saw Devin looking at him, he stood up, shifted on his feet, then sat back down. Devin looked left and right, but other than he and Cheryl, there was no one else in the lot.

"Cody. Where's Cody?" he said to Cheryl. "Did you see him leave?"

She shook her head. "He ran to the other side of the store."

Crap. Maybe he was cut. He could be bleeding to death.

Remembering what had happened to Karston because he'd waited too long, Devin turned back toward the door and started walking. Cheryl followed, but he whirled and ordered, "Get Ben and walk around front. Grab some cops and tell them what's going on!" he said.

A pained look flashed on her face. "No!" she said.

"Go!" Devin screamed back as if he were slapping her with the word. "Hurry!"

She nodded, whirled, and started trotting off toward Ben.

Cheryl would be safe. She had to be. But he couldn't leave Cody to that thing any more than he could abandon him to the two Slits, no matter how angry he was. He walked back to the door, desperately scanning the trash bins for a piece of wood or metal, anything he could use as a weapon.

He prayed it was gone. He prayed he could just get in and pull Cody out.

He pulled the rear door open as gently as he could and creeped back in. Once he reached the main room, he stood there, staring out the front windows. The mob swarming outside the club was huge, and not a single officer was visible among the mass of forms. He could see the swirling lights from the empty police cars, though; they were streaming into the store, weaving through the slats on the cribs, making the dangling stars and dolls cast long misshapen shadows everywhere. Any one of the shadows could be a monster. Who knew how long it would take Cheryl to get someone's attention?

"Cody?" he whispered into the black.

The other side. Cheryl said he'd gone to the other side. That was where all the racks and shelves of children's clothes were. As he passed the main entrance, he looked toward the back of the store toward the restrooms. Fluorescent light glowed from behind the cracked door of the men's room, but everything beyond it seemed quiet.

Maybe it was gone.

Devin took a few more steps. When his sneaker hit something sticky, he looked down at the linoleum. There was a trail of something thick and dark, like oil. He pushed at it with the toe of his sneaker, and it smeared easily. Blood. He closed his eyes, not wanting to believe that it was Cody's, but followed the trail nevertheless, moving softly from display case to display case. By the time it stopped, Devin had reached the far wall.

"Cody?" he whispered again. Before he could inhale after speaking, something lurched up behind him. Long fingers wrapped tightly around his skull and jaw. He felt his head yanked backward with incredible force. His body followed, but the pulling continued. Before he knew it, he was on the floor with a muscular figure leaning over him, something dripping from one of its long arms.

Cody.

"Cody, man . . ."

"Shhh!" Cody whispered. "It's still out there, over by the cribs. In the bathroom, I smacked it with my guitar. It was like slamming into a brick wall. I think I ruined the axe."

Devin recalled the splintered wood. "Yeah," he whispered, "I think you did."

Cody didn't seem to care. His eyes were crazed, glazed. He was terrified. Devin had never seen Cody like this, had never imagined he would. He rolled up and knelt beside Cody. They both held on to the sides of the cribs, looking out between the slats, watching for even a hint of movement.

"What do you think it is?" Devin whispered.

Cody looked at him and gave him a weaker version of his sneer. "Are you really that stupid? Can't you figure anything out? It's the thing from your damn song!"

The information felt like a slap. "No," Devin answered. "No way. The song was just a lullaby my grandmother sang to me when I was a baby."

"Yeah? Then your grandmother's a freaking witch," Cody hissed. He was bobbing back and forth, occasionally grabbing his arm and looking at the blood on his palm. "It's not stopping. I feel dizzy. Not good."

It looked like the big cut on his arm was the only damage, but there were so many dark stains on his shirt, Devin couldn't be sure. Cody looked out at the floor. "I say we make a run for it, dive for the front door, and hope it opens. If it doesn't, we can force it."

Devin shook his head. "The police will be here any second. Let's just wait!"

A bursting laugh of air flew from Cody's mouth. "You, always with the goddamn waiting. What if they don't? I'm going to pass out. It's thirty yards, man. Let's go!"

Devin stared at Cody's blue eyes. They were wavering. His head seemed to list on his neck. "I'm probably not going to get that door open without you," Cody said.

Devin counted his breaths. He kept hoping Cheryl and Ben had gotten someone's attention, that at any second those doors would burst open from the other side, the police would rush in, and they'd be saved.

But the only thing that happened was that Cody's eyes began to droop. As he held his arm, the blood seeped between his fingers and dripped onto the floor.

Devin tried to remember first aid, how to make a tourniquet. Could he do that?

He took another breath. Another thick drop of

Cody's blood fell.

"Okay," Devin finally said. "Let's go. On three."

The light in Cody's eyes seemed to flare. A slight smile went to his lips.

"See that?" he panted. "I keep telling Cheryl you're not so stupid."

"One . . ." Devin said, tensing. "Two . . ."

Before he could say *three* they were both running, stumbling across the children's clothing section toward the front door. Nothing else seemed to move except them. The beautiful glass double doors loomed closer and closer. The lights from outside grew brighter.

One second, Cody was beside him, even getting a little ahead; then there was a slight rush of air, and he was gone.

Devin stopped and whirled. Cody was on the floor, on his back, his arms above his head. He was moving. His arms looked wrong, too long. At once, Devin realized the thing was dragging him back into the depths of the store, away from the blinding light.

As Devin watched, it pulled Cody beneath a rack of footsie pajamas, the little cloth legs and feet parting to make way for the creature and its prey.

Devin turned and jumped after them. His feet

felt rubbery underneath him. The thing, along with Cody's torso, vanished beneath the rack.

There was a horrible snapping sound. Then Cody's powerful voice fell to screaming louder than Devin had ever heard it before. Just before Cody's feet vanished beneath the rack, Devin leaped across the floor and managed to grab one. He held the ankle, then the whole leg, bracing his feet against the linoleum and pulling as hard as he could.

"I've got you! I've got you!" he said, but he had no idea if Cody could hear him, because the cutting sound just grew louder. It was louder than the pounding rush in Devin's head, louder than Cody's screams, which peaked, then faded into nothing.

For a second, for one brief instant, all of Devin's pulling and yanking seemed to pay off. The leg came free in his arms. But Cody was no longer attached.

As the police burst through the front door, filling the darkness with the beams of their flashlights, Devin, his mind collapsing, could think only one thing:

Cody had been Torn.

The police grilled them for hours.

"Are you sure that's what you saw?"

"Was it like the monster in your song?"

"One kid died and your song got popular, right? Did you think your song would get even more popular if someone else died, too? Did you think it would be cool?"

Terms like "satan worship" and "cult sacrifice" were bandied about, making Devin fearful, frustrated, and ultimately angry. He worried that if they had dressed in trench coats or in Goth style they'd have been charged and convicted on the basis of fashion. He realized grimly that misunderstanding and suspicion were just as much part of the long-standing legend of rock as the fame and the money.

He wished Cody were here. Cody would love to see how much the police were freaking out, how desperate they were to find anything that would give the slaughter some kind of sense, some kind of order. He imagined Cody laughing at them, making up stories just for fun.

Yes, officer, we worship a fish god who lives in a giant lair beneath the sea. Your so-called goldfish-bowl castles are a mere echo of our god's home. It does crave human blood at times....

Or the more familiar: *The music made me do it. Voices in the song told me to kill our lead guitarist, so I figured, hey, what the hell. I mean, wouldn't you?*

It would be so simple to get them to believe anything. Anything except the truth. But that, Devin had to admit, sounded, even to him, even now, in the cold light of the small room they kept him in, the strangest of all.

One Word Ben was the first to be released, either because he was the only one who didn't claim to see a monster, or because his one-word answers made things go faster. Cheryl was second.

She was hysterical, and she'd only caught a glimpse of the thing in the men's room, so her description was easily dismissed, both by the police and by her.

But Devin—Devin was the only witness to the actual murder. The only witness to both murders, and the only one who insisted on what he saw, who described it in unbelievable detail.

So they tested him for drugs, but since the results would take days, they grilled him for hours more, then tested him again in case they would be unhappy with the results from the first tests. Then they had a psychiatrist speak to him. Then they grilled him some more.

They wanted very badly to press charges, but when the crime scene photos and forensics came back, showing the hole in the bathroom ceiling, the shattered guitar, the thick scratch marks on the floor and walls, and the sheer strength needed to rip Cody's leg off, they corroborated his story. And when Devin's father, looking older and smaller than he'd ever seemed before, bellowed and threatened to sue, the detectives finally conceded that "something like" what Devin described might actually have occurred.

But on the way out, as if Devin couldn't hear, they advised his father of their various theories: that the killer had threatened Devin in some way so that he was unwilling to give honest testimony, or that he was on drugs, or that he was crazy. When his father pushed, though, they admitted they couldn't prove any of that. So, yes, they'd let him go, for now, but they wanted to know his whereabouts 24/7.

The car ride home was shorter but more grueling than his time at the station. His dad babbled about Columbine and asked him over and over about drugs, about gangs, about guns. The sharp, steady man had never seemed so clueless before, never felt so far away.

As they drove, the morning light seeping between the trees felt as brittle as Devin's tired head. His sinuses were on fire. He had some sort of cold, maybe a fever.

It was only when his mother hugged him, warm and soft in a housecoat she'd worn since he was a child, that Devin realized how cold and stiff he felt. She looked at him, brushed his hair out of his face, and then quickly made an excuse to vanish into the kitchen to get him something hot to eat. They would talk later, after he'd rested. After she'd had a nervous breakdown or two.

Devin plodded up the stairs, entered the hallway bathroom, stripped off his clothes, and tossed them on the floor. Seeing the blotches of dried blood on the pants and shirt made him dizzy, but he managed to stumble into the shower. The burst of warm water soothed his skin and forced his shoulder muscles to relax; yet even though he stood there for a long time, something in him still stayed cold.

Cody was dead. Karston had been a blow, but Cody was different. He was more like a force of nature, and forces of nature shouldn't die.

Until that moment, when Devin felt as if a part of himself was missing, he never realized how much he both hated Cody and loved him, how much he thought he was a jerk, an asshole, yet shared Cody's opinion of himself, that he was some kind of god.

Devin stepped out of the shower. The sound of his parents arguing downstairs floated up through the heating vents. Their harsh whispers were short, angry, desperate. The details of the grudge match flew past him. He couldn't care less. He went into his room and closed the door, silencing them.

He threw himself back on his bed and stared at the ceiling. Eventually, he looked out the large window, where he caught the tops of the trees shifting in a hard wind. The woods seemed to go on forever.

A greater truth had suddenly opened up for Devin. It sat there in front of him, thick and black, utterly unknown and waiting to swallow him whole: a monster.

A monster had killed Karston and Cody. Not some wacky deformed homeless guy with a hatchet—a for-real, beyond-the-ken-of-mortal-understanding monster, or whatever you wanted to call something so strong you could shatter a solid body Les Paul against it without even slowing it down.

And it looked so damn familiar.

Even now he wanted to look under his bed, to make sure it wasn't there.

Could it really have come from the song like Cody said? How screwed up was that? Was it created by the song, or did the song "call" to it? What were the rules? *Were* there any rules? Did it only take bad children? Was he safe? He didn't feel safe.

Was Cheryl safe? Was One Word Ben?

Cheryl. The last time he'd seen her was when her parents took her out of the station. Her beautiful smooth skin was totally white, and there were deep red circles under her eyes. He had called to her, but she'd been far down the hall, being pulled into one of the interrogation rooms.

He grabbed his cell and punched her number on the speed dial.

"Hey," she said in a flash. She sounded tired, as if he'd woken her.

"Hey," he said back. "How are you?"

"Horrible."

"Me, too. Your parents ever going to let you out of the house again?"

"I hope not. Yours?"

"Downstairs fighting about something. I don't know who's going to win."

"Did you talk to Cody's family?"

Devin was surprised by the question. "No. I just got back."

"I want to call, but I'm scared. Like it would make it more real." Her voice was cracking. After a silence, she asked, "Was it real?"

Devin thought about it a second and said, "Yes."

"What are we going to do?"

"I don't know."

There was a longer pause, but Devin didn't think of hanging up. The silence was fine. Just knowing she was on the other end, despite the space between them, felt good.

After a while, Cheryl broke the silence. "It's all over the chat rooms, you know. They're thinking of canceling school Monday. There's a radio station playing the song, creeping people out. There's a video clip Judy sent me from the club. It's got a great shot of . . . Cody . . . singing . . . and there's more of those dust dots flying around."

More silence.

"Maybe you should see it," Cheryl said. "I'll send it to you."

Devin stood, walked to his laptop, and woke it. "I'll take a look," he said. "What do you think they are?"

"I don't know. Maybe the angels from the song, the ones we're supposed to lie to. Maybe Cody didn't lie well enough," she answered.

The e-mail was already in his in-box. With a click, the large video file started downloading.

He smiled a little. "You kidding? Cody was a great liar."

"Yeah," she said. Her voice cracked and trailed off. She started crying.

"It's okay," he said. "I'd cry, too, but I'm too tired."

"It's not . . . it's not just that he's dead," she said.

"Then what?"

"I don't want to lie anymore either. There's something I have to tell you. I'm so sorry I didn't tell you before. You're so . . . good."

He could feel her trying to pull herself together.

"What? What is it? Don't leave me hanging."

Her voice was halting. "No. Not now. I have to do it in person."

He felt himself getting angry. He didn't want to be angry—not now, not at her—but he felt it anyway. "No, just tell me. My brain is screwed up enough as it is."

A pause, and then, "You'll hate me."

What the hell is she talking about?

"I couldn't, Cheryl, not you."

"You could. It's about me and Cody."

Silence. Devin felt that abyss open up in front

159

of him again. The one that held the darker truths.

"We were together. After Karston died. Just once."

Now it was Devin's turn to fall silent.

"Devin? Are you there?" Cheryl said. "I need to hear your voice right now. I'm so scared. I just felt like I was lying to you and . . ."

Lying to the angels . . .

"I've got to go," Devin said flatly.

"No, please. I need to talk to you."

A feeling like a million fire ants chewing at his gut rose up in him.

"Yeah, well, right now I need some time," he said. He felt cruel. He didn't care. He pressed End and flung the phone into his bed, where it landed soundlessly against the folds of the bedspread.

It made sense, damn it. It made total sense. Cody was, well, Cody. Friendship or loyalty wouldn't hold him back. It was Cheryl who was looking different to him now.

Two crooks and a slut . . .

The sound of his parents' battle rose through the vents in his room. Shaking, Devin lay down on his bed, put his head in a pillow, and screamed. Once, twice, then when the third scream ripped his throat raw, he stopped.

Through the pillow, he heard his ring tone. Cheryl was trying to call him back. He turned the phone off, and the little light showing Cheryl's number went dead. There was another beep from across the room, from his laptop. An image of Tunnel Vision filled the screen. Cody's voice came through the speakers, low, harsh, and pointed:

> *No one's pure, my love, love, love,*
> *But if you cross the line,*
> *Your deeds will call out to the wild,*
> *And there won't be much time.*

Karston had stolen money from him. Cody had been amoral at best. Now Cheryl had cheated on him. That much of the song was right, no one was pure. But did it mean they were all condemned? What rules did the monster follow?

Monster. Maybe it was *him*. Maybe all the years he'd spent "straddling the fence" as Cody called it had welled up and out of him as this weird id-thing. Or maybe at least one of all the police theories was right, maybe Devin was psychotic, killing Karston and Cody himself and not remembering.

Curious, he got up and stepped closer to the screen, watching Cody twist in an impassioned performance with the rest of them dutifully backing. Cheryl was right; the dots were there again. They were swirling around Cody, focusing on his head, twirling frantically as if trying to get his attention.

The camera zoomed in for a close-up of the lead singer. Cody's rough, handsome face filled the screen. The dots were still there, clearer now as they circled his mouth, his lips, the mike, the sources of the sound. There were ten, maybe fifteen, little transparent dots of light.

As he came to the end, they froze, and all at once flew away, as if it was too late and whatever it was they were trying to warn about would happen anyway.

Devin stopped the clip, backed it up, and played it again. Yeah, the specks were dancing around Cody, right until the end of the last verse. Then they took off, like little bats out of little hell.

First it had been him and Karston. Karston died. Now it was Cody and Cody died. What would the police make of this, he wondered? Dust. Same thing he would have before he'd seen the beast.

There were no dots dancing around him, though. None around One Word Ben. What about Cheryl? It was hard to say; she was furthest back in the shot, and there weren't many close-ups.

He froze the screen and clicked through a frame at a time. It was digital video, and from a good camera, too, so the image was pretty clean. He tried to find a clear frame with Cheryl in it. Once he did, he captured the screen and opened it in his image editor. Using the magnifier tool, he zoomed in. There they were, circling her mouth, her head, her ears, as if infesting her with death.

Cheryl. Karston. Cody. Cheryl.

He zoomed in tighter. The image pixelated, broke up into little squares of different color and shading, but the light and dark still conspired to create an image. It wasn't a clear picture exactly, more something that might be there or might not, like the face of the man in the moon.

Only this face didn't look like the man in the moon.

It looked like Karston.

Devin's parents couldn't understand why, now of all times, he was suddenly so desperate to see Namana. They tried to put him off, fearful it was another sign of some hidden mental problem, or that the frantic, traumatized teen would just upset the fragile old woman.

His mother and father fought twice over it, long and hard, finally agreeing to forbid him, but Devin kept insisting, repeatedly and uncharacteristically. He didn't whine about it like a child; he demanded it, in a tone of voice they'd never heard from him before.

So finally they relented, on the condition his father drive.

"You're too upset for one, and we're damned if we're going to leave you alone again for a while," his dad explained. He phoned the police, as he'd been instructed, to tell them where they'd be the next morning.

They'd planned on leaving at nine A.M., but the police called to ask for more details and phone numbers, which delayed their departure until nine thirty. Finally, his dad, his face a mask, stiffly tossed a file stuffed with papers onto the floor of the SUV's passenger seat. He started the engine and wordlessly waited for Devin to climb in and put on his seat belt. They pulled out of the gated community, his father doing the speed limit, not a mile more or a mile less. Just the limit, as if every cop in the world were watching them.

In silence, they drove past the suburbs into the downtrodden industrial section of town, which was filled with old factories and rundown homes. It was only when they reached the interstate and the view of flat, square buildings surrendered to green, rounded hills that the invisible bond with Macy, and all its tensions and horrors, seemed to weaken just a bit.

His dad's face softened, but the muscle beneath

his right eye twitched. He blinked a few times too often, cleared his throat, and asked, with embarrassment, some pointless question about how comfortable Devin was in his seat, and if he'd managed to get any sleep.

Devin suddenly knew that what he had thought of as his father's anger was really a kind of helpless fear. He wanted to pat his father on the shoulder, tell him what a great job he'd done raising his son, that his son was all right, and that everything was going to be okay.

But everything wasn't going to be okay, so he couldn't.

Eventually, his father broke the silence again. "There are things we have to talk about."

"Age before beauty," Devin said. It was an old line between them. His father smiled, remembering.

"Two big things. First, I've decided to request a transfer to San Diego. We're going to put the house up. It'll mean some big changes, like a smaller house, but . . ."

Devin stared.

He should have seen that one coming. His mother had been begging to leave for years. She had family in California. The schools were better there, she insisted, and there were more opportunities. His father had almost given in about a year and a half ago. Devin hadn't been doing so well in school, but then the band formed and both his parents were happy to see him so involved. His father had probably hoped the issue was buried forever. But now, no more Macy. *California, here we come.*

His father kept talking, as if he had to explain why he'd given in.

"Your mother was right," he said. "I just didn't see it. Macy's been dying for years. Now it's just gone to hell and it's sucking us down with it. They don't even have gang slayings like that in New York. I'm only sorry I let us stay here so long. That's my fault."

"You don't have to . . . ," Devin started to say. He understood. Part of him hoped that whatever he'd unleashed wouldn't be able to travel that far.

"There's something else," his father said. "It's a little harder to . . . to talk about."

Devin's brow furrowed. *What?*

The emotion began to drain from his father's face. The mask returned. He was bracing himself.

"After all that's happened, and hell, we don't

even know *what* happened, but your mother and I . . . well, maybe it would be best . . . maybe you should just . . . look inside the folder," he said.

Devin reached down and lifted the straw-colored file. It was thick with paper. Inside were a series of color Web page printouts. Images sprinkled among the text showed happy teens engaged in sports and other wholesome activities as they played on lush green fields with new equipment beneath a perfect blue sky. Other images showed the teens accepting guidance from older, wiser adults. Everyone smiled. Everyone was pleasant. Everyone was healthy.

Devin flipped through the pages. There were about twenty. Some had the perfection of their layout marred by handwritten notes from his father, and certain sections were highlighted in yellow. It still took a moment for Devin to register what he was looking at. They were ads for the rich kids' version of drug rehab centers—behavior modification camps.

Devin stared, mouth open wide. His father exhaled and started talking again.

"It's something we need to think about. Some of them look pretty nice. You'd have Internet access, a DVD player. We were thinking you could start maybe next week, avoid all the mess of moving, then meet us in San Diego later, start there with a clean slate."

If Devin's father were expecting some kind of fight, he didn't get it. Instead Devin just laughed. It was a dismissive, derisive laugh that mushroomed uncontrollably into a ghoulish cackle. At the end of it, Devin just shook his head. "You know, Dad, I've never taken any drugs, but I sure as hell am thinking about it now."

"Don't talk like that," his father said.

So he didn't. He didn't say anything for the rest of the drive.

The Daybridge Senior Care Facility looked just like the bright and shiny institutions in the folder his dad had dutifully prepared. It all seemed so clean, until they walked into the well-lit, tastefully decorated lobby and the smells Devin associated with old people filled the air. Dried skin dying too quickly. Sweet food mashed up so that it was easy to chew. A whiff of some gross cleaning fluid that didn't mask the other smells.

Devin signed in at the counter. He turned to

give his father the pen, but his old man shook his head. "No, Devin. I can't see her. After you . . . after what happened yesterday, I'm just too drained. Half the time she doesn't recognize me anyway. I'll wait here."

Devin looked at him, wondering if there'd ever be a time he wouldn't want to see his own parent because it was too draining. Then, realizing he already felt that way about both of his parents, he just nodded. It would be easier to talk to Namana alone.

To the right of the counter was a large white door with a little window in the center and a serious metal lock and plate on the side. As Devin was buzzed in, his father called to him. "Don't say anything to upset her."

Devin pretended not to hear. If his father wanted to issue orders, he should have come along. Alone, Devin entered the white corridor and let the door click shut behind him. The old-people smell was stronger, but the view was more pleasant because the hall opened up into a wide, sunny space. As he walked forward, he saw an angled ceiling that was nearly all glass and filled the room with natural sunlight. There were plants on either side of every lounge chair, more standing against the support columns, and even a few small trees, giving the area a natural, open feel.

A few of the residents occupied some of the chairs. Some played chess; others read. One tall bald man wore what looked like a hospital gown. He leaned against a pillar like he was one of the trees, a white birch. His eyes were vacant, and he moaned softly as mucous dripped in a long viscous strand from his nose, halfway down his chest.

Devin tried not to stare. Or inhale. He stepped slowly into the center of the room. Some of the women looked at him and whispered to one another. They giggled and tried to catch his eye. It was utterly gross to think they were flirting with him, so he forced himself to assume they were just being friendly. He scanned their faces. It'd been maybe three years since he'd seen Namana. He wasn't sure how much she might change in that time. Could one of these women even *be* her?

He was about to speak to one of the gigglers when a uniformed nurse appeared at the far end of the room, guiding a small, snow-white-haired resident with a walker. The last time he'd seen Namana, her hair had still been gray mixed with a

171

few strands of black, and she'd been heavier. This frail woman looked more like someone had started making a life-size Namana doll, but had run out of material. It was her, though.

He walked up and smiled as sincerely as he could, reminding himself of Cody on stage. "Hi, Namana, how are you?"

She twisted her head slightly and looked at him, then moved her hand in a spastic twitching motion, as if waving him away. Her hand moved at the wrist, but her fingers dangled lifelessly. There was a blue bruise on the back of her left hand, from some IV needle or another.

She continued waving, but the smiling nurse helped her into a chair, laying her down like a blanket on top of the thick cushions. The nurse put the walker against the wall and said, with what seemed an inappropriate amount of energy, "There! All set!"

Devin came closer. Namana raised her head. Her blue eyes were hazy behind the thick glasses, but now at least they seemed to really focus on him. She scrunched her eyebrows a moment, as if trying to place Devin's face.

The nurse leaned down till she was right next

to his grandmother's ear and said loudly, "This is your grandson! Devin! He's come to see you!"

Namana bobbed her head slightly. She agreed.

The nurse turned to Devin with a wide smile. "Sometimes she forgets," she said in a pleasant stage whisper. "I'll leave you two alone. Call me if you need anything. I'm Angie."

"Thanks," Devin said. Angie spun and walked away.

He looked at his grandmother, wondering if the whole trip had been a waste, if there were anything at all she'd be able to tell him. Surprisingly, her hand again dangling from her wrist, Namana waved him closer.

"What is it, Namana?" he said, putting his head nearer. He was still about a foot away, nervous. Even after everything he'd been through—maybe because of it—he was afraid of her because she was so old. She waved him closer still. He complied, by inches, until he was just close enough for her to grab him hard by the back of his head.

He was surprised by how strong she was. Her grasp made him feel like a child too weak in body and soul to resist as she pulled his face down to hers. They touched, nose to nose. Then, she didn't so much kiss his cheek as make a soft *pup-pup* sound with her smacking lips near his skin.

"Devin," she said softly, as if it were the answer to a test question that had been plaguing her.

"Namana," he said, and hugged her gently. As he pulled back, he saw her eyes fill with tears. Guilt rushed up inside him for not seeing her for so long. There was a tissue box on a table next to the chair. He pulled out a sheet and patted her wet cheeks with it. She bristled, grabbed the tissue, and pushed her glasses up and out of the way so she could use it to dab her eyes.

"Sorry," he said.

"I'll do it," she croaked. "I'll do it. You're a baby. Shouldn't have to . . ."

Devin managed a bitter little smile. "Not exactly a baby anymore, Namana."

She narrowed her gaze at him, trying to focus on his features. "No, you're not," she said sadly. She leaned forward a little and added conspiratorially, "Neither am I."

They both laughed. Devin felt grateful he could still recognize her.

Now came the hard part. The reason for the visit. He didn't want to "upset her," as his father said, but he had to find out what she might know about the creature.

"Namana, do you remember that song you used to sing me, to put me to sleep?" he said. "When I was a baby?"

A sweet smile spread on her lips. She started humming, then she closed her eyes and put her arms out in front of her, as if recalling what a child in her lap felt like.

As he listened, the years crumbled, and Devin remembered what it was like to sit with her, feeling warm and snug as she sang, holding something in his hands, some stuffed toy made of dark fur. A teddy bear?

He was surprised and embarrassed at how well he'd remembered the melody. He'd been thinking he'd made more of it up, but as she hummed, he realized he'd reproduced it note for note, word for word. Another illusion came crumbling down as he realized he was no musical genius, he'd stolen the song whole hog.

"*Lay still, still, still,*" she croaked. Her voice wasn't harsh at all, the way he remembered it; it was gentle, soothing. At least it was now.

If it wasn't his song, whose was it?

There was something compelling in the melody, something that made everyone who heard it speechless for a few moments. Maybe that was part of its magic, that the song would stay in your mind, and then force its way out again. Was that why he remembered it so precisely? It explained why he felt drawn to it, why his usual ambivalence had vanished when he'd sung it at the last show.

"Namana," he said, but she kept singing. He said it a little louder, "Namana?"

"Eh?" The spell was broken. She was back in the room.

"The song. Where did it come from?"

She gave him a dreamy, demented smile. "From mommas and grandmommas singing to their babies."

He shook his head. "No, I mean where did *you* learn it?"

"Oh. Well, when I was a girl, my great-grand-mother used to sing it to me. No one liked her very much. She was good to those she loved. Not to those she didn't."

"Was she a witch? Was your great-grandma magic?"

Namana shook her head. "No." Then she thought

better of her answer. "Maybe. I don't really remember. I just remember she loved me. And that she was *very* old. Older than I am now. They didn't like her, though."

"Who didn't like her?"

"People in the town. You can't like everyone. She had her ways."

"The thing in the song—did the people in the town think it was real?"

She went quiet. Her eyes were closed for so long Devin was afraid she'd fallen asleep. His memory again flashed to the toy he had held in his hands. He'd never had a teddy bear. What was it?

He was about to repeat the question when she leaned forward and whispered, "It comes with the song."

Devin's heart started beating faster. She knew. Maybe she could help. "Why, Namana? Why does it come with the song?"

She made a light gargling sound and managed a shrug of her thin shoulders. "I don't know. Maybe it likes the song. Wouldn't you like a pretty song that was about you?" Her eyes twinkled with a light he remembered from long ago.

Is she joking with me? Is this a game she

thinks we're playing?

"No, Namana, tell me. It's important. It's so important."

She picked her hands up and her fingers danced a little in the air between them, acting out the beast's movements as she spoke. "It comes to take revenge against people who've been bad to you. It comes to whoever sings it just right. It looks around at whoever called it, into their heart, and sees who they think has been bad. Then it gets them, gets every last one they think is bad. That's why people never liked my great-grandma. She thought a lot of them were bad."

Devin's head was swimming. *Whoever sings it?*

It suddenly made horrible sense. Devin had summoned it. It'd killed Karston because he'd stolen money from Devin, Cody because Devin was disgusted with his behavior. And now it would come for . . . Cheryl?

An image of the thing's long arms, wrapping its claws into her long hair filled his head, its sharp teeth and squat face looking oh so familiar.

Oh no. He could practically feel it in his hands. The toy, the furry toy he cradled in his hands when Namana sang to him. It wasn't a teddy bear.

He liked monsters, even as a toddler. He had a grotesque stupid little monster doll, with short legs, long arms, and a batlike face. And he loved it because it scared him so much. Rotted and broken, the pieces had been thrown out a few weeks ago, along with his robot collection.

"Why does it look like that?" he said, more to himself than his grandmother.

"It looks like whatever you want it to. Whatever you think is most horrible," she said calmly.

It's me. I made it. I called it. Even onstage, Cody was riffing, but I sang the melody straight. And the little lights danced around Cody's and Cheryl's heads.

His face dropped. He felt himself going pale.

"Namana," he whispered. "Why would you ever sing such a song?"

She chuckled and nodded her head. "To remind you to always be good. But you never had anything to worry about, Devin. I *always* thought you were good."

She narrowed her eyes again and made her voice low. "All babies are good. It's only when they get older they're bad." She chuckled at that, maybe remembering her own misspent youth. "Then," she

179

concluded, "they're *all* bad!"

Her hands rose and she jabbed her index fingers, stabbing little points in the air. "And the spirits of the dead hear the song, too. They come and try to warn whoever's singing. Stop, stop, stop, they say, with their little mouths and their little hands, but no one ever listens. No one hears them. They're just too small for this world. Too small and worn out, like your old Namana."

Devin exhaled and leaned closer, making sure she was looking him in the eye.

"Namana, this is important. Is there any way to destroy it? To stop it?"

She smacked her dry lips twice and moaned a little before speaking. "Look at my hand," she said, raising it between them both. Her eyes widened as she marveled at her own body. "All old and wrinkled. This is what a hand does if you keep it around long enough. Hands get wrinkled. Children go bad. That's it. That's all."

Devin felt himself getting frantic.

"What about what it says in the song? What if you lie to the angels? Does that mean something? Anything? Can they help?"

She puckered her wrinkled lips and shook her

head. "Pht. No, no, no. That wasn't in the song. I made that part up so you wouldn't get *too* scared. There's no way to stop it. It just likes the song. It likes being sung about."

Devin's face must have registered his agony, because she reached out and patted him on the cheek. "But don't *you* worry. *You're* a good boy."

"I have to go," he said. He stood sharply, but Namana moved faster and grabbed his arm. There was so little muscle to her fingers he could feel the bones dig into his flesh, as if they were claws. Instinctively, he tried to pull away, but her grip was so tight he nearly lifted her whole body out of the chair.

"A *good* boy!" she said, over and over again.

The next day, despite his plans to attend Cody's wake at four o'clock, after a quiet time at home Devin McCloud went missing. He'd taken his parents' SUV, all the cash in the house, clothes, and some of his music equipment. There was no note left behind, no nothing. The police pretended to commiserate with his distraught parents, but really, they were now convinced he had something to do with the murders.

He himself also now knew that he did. For a while, he hoped maybe he *was* crazy like they thought, that maybe he had killed Cody and Karston and only imagined the creature. It didn't matter anymore. The solution was the same.

By sunset, Devin sat on a certain large rock just outside Macy, where he watched a yellow band of dying sun as it shone between the upper branches of a row of tall trees. This was where he and Cheryl met when they couldn't find anyplace else to be alone, back when they were together, which seemed so long ago. He was confident his parents and the police wouldn't think to look here, at least for what he hoped would be more than enough time.

At his back, half-built McMansions peeked through the thinner woods that sat along the dirt road, but here was where construction had stopped. The swelling suburbs behind him, he faced a forest where birds chirped and squirrels rustled in the trees. It was a light, cheerful sound.

The SUV was parked as close to the rock as he could get it, engine idling. His Ovation was on his lap, plugged into a practice amp. He plucked the strings of his guitar and sang:

Sun is low, the sky gray, gray, gray,
All day's colors gone,
Your heart beats slowly, drowsy eyes,
Soon your dreams will come.

He sang as best he could, inhaling hard and breathing out slow in an effort to get the low notes just right. He wasn't Cody, but, he thought with some strange pleasure, that he came pretty close.

He had to summon it here, or else it would be coming for Cheryl soon. He had seen the dots swirling around her head in the video. The spirits must've known she was cheating on him, tried to warn her even then. And the MP3 of the club gig was making its way across the Internet, with Devin's recorded voice calling to the creature again and again. It was only a matter of time. He had to stop it. He couldn't let her die. Or anyone else who happened to earn his anger while the song was on the air. This was the only thing he could think to do, to hold up some bright and shiny object to lure it away.

Himself.

Would it work? It followed the song and took revenge on whoever the singer hated. Now that Devin hated himself for causing the death of his friends, by rights it should follow him. That should be enough, shouldn't it? His only worry echoed a question Cody had asked him so long ago: Was he bad enough to be worth its while?

A branch snapped. He stopped playing. It might've been the wind, but he couldn't be sure. With his eyes he again measured the distance to the SUV. Could he make it to the driver's seat? Get the car in gear and gun it before the thing reached him?

Sure. Sure he could. Then he'd drive, fast and hard, as long as he could, with his giant monster toy chasing him. He could take it to the middle of a city where everyone could see, or a military base where they've got the big guns, or the desert where neither of them would ever be seen again.

Just so long as he could take it somewhere away from Cheryl.

He wasn't even sure he'd forgiven her for Cody. He only knew he didn't want her to die.

When the cracking sound failed to come again, Devin figured it really was just the wind, and went back to his playing. As he sat there, strumming, singing, he thought he felt the little spirits around him, tickling his skin, trying to pull him away with their weak, ethereal hands and vain pleas. He imagined Cody among them now and thought he knew what he would say. While the others would be screaming, "No! Stop! Run away!" Cody would be there, away from the crowd, bopping his head, saying, "Yeah, man, go ahead. Do it. DO IT!"

Don't start, sweet child, lay still, still, still.
Angels on their way
Will ride the breeze tonight to ask
If you were good today.

No further cracking came, but a minute later a car engine whirred behind him. Tires crunched on the dirt. The police?

He spun. No, no, no. Worse. Cheryl's little red Civic pulled up beside his SUV. Of course she knew where he'd be. Crap. Why'd he picked this place? Did some stupid selfish psychotic part of himself want her to find him? He had to get rid of her, fast.

Really fast.

Their eyes met through the windshield. She got out. She was wearing the same black dress she'd worn at Karston's funeral, the one that looked too good on her.

The band of yellow light was gone by now, replaced with something redder, dimmer. A chill filled the air. Cheryl pulled her sweater tightly around her shoulders as she spoke. "Devin, what are you doing here? Everyone's looking for you.

The police, too."

Devin stood atop the rock and waved her back.

"You've got to get out of here," he said. "You've got to get out of here now."

She looked in the back of the SUV, saw the red plastic containers. Her nostrils flared at the smell. "Is that gasoline? What are you doing with all that gasoline in the back of your car?"

"Once I get going, I can't afford to stop. I've got to lead it out of here," he said. "It's coming again, Cheryl. It's coming for you. Because you were bad."

Her eyes went wide. "Devin! Stop it! That's crazy! You're scaring me."

Now it was his turn to look shocked. "What? Karston and Cody are dead and you're just getting scared now? You *saw* it. You know what it can do. I've got to do this before it gets *you*! Now, go!"

She twisted her head back and forth as if trying to shake out the words. "Stop it! I don't know what I saw! It was dark! I know I started this whole thing with the stupid video, but it's just dust, like you said! I thought it was cool, I thought it would be good for the band, so I uploaded it and started the rumor! But, really, it . . . it could have been a Slit or a psycho, like the police said! They'll catch him and everything will be fine again!"

So you lied about that, too, Devin thought.

When his face remained grim, she tried another tack. "I'm sorry about that. I'm sorry about me and Cody, I'm so sorry, but it happened, okay? You've got to get out of this crazy fantasy and come home! I feel like I've been living in a nightmare and I just want to wake up, okay? I want us both to wake up!"

Devin shook his head. "It's real. The song called it. It comes and then it kills whoever I think is bad. Karston stole some money from me and Cody, well, Cody was an asshole. And you . . . you cheated on me," Devin said.

She took a step back, perhaps frightened by something she saw in his eyes. "Devin," she said, "you're not taking meth or anything, are you? Maybe even just pot?"

Devin didn't bother answering.

As if a cosmic switch had been flipped, the wind in the trees died. The chattering of the birds and squirrels stopped. Deep in the woods, branches cracked. Not one, like before, but one after another. It was coming.

"You've got to get out of here," Devin said, hopping off the rock near her.

"No," Cheryl said, taking out her cell. "You need

help. I'm calling your parents and I'm telling them where you are."

In a flash, Devin closed the distance between them and slammed the cell phone out of her hand. It landed in the grass, its light glowing for a moment before dying.

The crunching branches grew louder. Cheryl snapped her head toward the woods. Devin was strangely relieved that she heard it, too. She pulled at his shoulders, trying one last time to be the bright shiny thing that distracted him. "I won't leave you! I'll go with you!"

The next branch snapped somewhere very nearby.

A horrible thought came to Devin. He'd sung the song to call it to himself, but even so, Cheryl was here now. What if it still went after her? Did he really think he was bad enough?

Cheryl looked at him again, eyes wide and sad and said, "Please."

She came forward. He felt his body pull toward her, wanting to hold her, to run with her. Could she come?

No. He had to get off the fence and for once in his life decide, or she would be dead. So he decided.

He decided to be bad.

He pulled his arm back and slapped her, as hard as he could, across the face. Then he pulled back and hit her again, harder.

"GET OUT OF HERE!" he screamed, truly hating himself.

She stumbled backward, stunned. She looked at him. Her face scrunched up as if she were going to cry, but she stopped herself, no longer willing to seem vulnerable in front of him.

He didn't give her a second to react. He came forward, screaming, slapping her, punching her, pushing her back toward her car.

Am I bad enough yet? Am I bad enough now? he thought as he pummeled her.

She gasped, shielded herself, ran back to her car and closed the door. He pounded on the glass, on the windshield, howling wildly, trying to make himself as much a monster as he could, as she, near hysteria, fumbled for her keys.

A loud snap, maybe ten yards away, finally stopped him. He caught a glimpse of a long-armed shadow slipping among the trees. Without even casting Cheryl a final glance, Devin leaped into his SUV, gunned the engine, and spun it toward the sounds.

Am I bad enough now?

At once, something leaped from the woods, out onto the hood, its arms, impossibly, nearly twice as long as its legs. It smashed its thick claws down, but the car lurched forward, sending it sprawling over the roof and onto the dirt road.

Devin threw the SUV into reverse and slammed into it. It felt like he'd damaged the car. The thing howled, maybe in pain, making a sound like the wind, then jumped at the SUV again. The big car spun on the dirt road and moved forward, slowly at first. Devin wanted to make sure the thing would follow. When it did, Devin sped up, pushing the gas pedal, bit by bit, to the floor.

Inside the Civic, head and body aching, heart shredded, Cheryl wiped the blood from her lips and watched the SUV race away. A dark and hungry thing ripped along behind it, pulling itself with long arms as it leaped—no, flew—from tree to tree, not quite catching up, not quite falling behind.

As long as she could, Cheryl followed with teary eyes as the thing chased the sleek car into the jagged shades of blackness as Devin passed completely through the forest's edge.

EPILOGUE

In Lockwood Orphanage . . .

Down the shadowed halls and far above the classroom where Daphne and Shirley sat enraptured by Mary's tale . . .

Anne stumbled out of the Red Room, her face streaked with tears. She felt weak and confused. So much of the dread of that place still filled her head. The Headmistress held the door for her, a look of cruel satisfaction carved on her face.

"Not so smart now, are you?" the terrifying woman asked.

Anne didn't answer. She couldn't. She heard the words, but the moment they entered her mind, they were swept away in a scarlet tide. Amid this rushing horror, her own thoughts began to emerge:

Headmistress . . . Shirley . . . big-mouthed Shirley . . . her fault . . . all her fault . . . they didn't come for me . . . Daphne, Mary . . . They let her drag me away . . . the bones . . . Where are the bones? . . . my turn to hide the bones . . .

A final, horrible remnant of the Red Room, an indescribable terror trapped behind that door with her, flashed through her memory. Anne cried out, swatting the air with her hands.

Then, the memory was gone.

"Damn," Anne whispered. "That *so* sucked."

"Where are your little friends, now?" the Headmistress asked, peering down all superior and pleased. "They didn't lift a finger to help you. And look, they didn't even come to see if you were well, after such a difficult night."

"They're not my friends," Anne said. "I'm trapped here with them, just like I'm trapped here with you. We're just flies in the same jar."

"As long as you hold no illusions about their loyalty," the Headmistress said. "At least with me, there is no pretense."

Yeah, like we're gonna bond, Anne thought. "Can I go, now?"

"Yes. I'm quite done with you." With that, the Headmistress broke apart into a cloud of sooty vapor. It spread out, rising to the shadowy ceiling, then vanished.

Anne moved shakily down the corridor. She wanted to find the other girls, or more precisely, wanted to find the bones. It was her night to hide them. For one night, they were hers, and no way she was going to let Shirley or Mary or Daphne snag the opportunity.

They wouldn't even have the bones anymore if it weren't for Anne. She'd seen daydreaming Mary drop her butt down to cover them when the Headmistress arrived. If Anne hadn't gotten all up in the Headmistress's grill, they would have been totally busted. Right now, they'd all be crying over the loss of their precious little bones. Game over.

She only acknowledged a hint of selfishness in this act. Yes, she was also concerned about losing the bones to the Headmistress. No way was she going to spend the rest of eternity in this place with those lame-ass freaks, and the bones, the stories, were her only way out. So yeah, she was protecting her own interests, but the other girls benefited from it. And . . .

They didn't even come to see if you were well, after such a difficult night.

"Bitches," Anne whispered.

For as long as she'd been with them—and god knew it seemed like an eternity already—they'd never once made her feel like she belonged. Always the outsider. Always wrong.

She walked through the decrepit halls, her mood worsening with each step. The memories of the Red Room were already shoved deep in a cell at the back of her mind, but the fear remained and blossomed into rage. She was furious with the three girls: the ungrateful brats.

Just wait until I find them.

In the classroom, Shirley and Daphne looked at the other girl as the final words of the tale left her lips.

Mary lowered her head, exhausted. Her hands gripped the desk in front of her tightly, her body arched over its flat surface. Wind moaned through the hole in the window. The paper map click-clicked against the wall.

"Well, that was a rip snorter," Daphne said.

"But Mary sang the song," Shirley added nervously. "What if she summoned that terrible thing?"

"It's just a story, kid."

"You don't know that," Shirley whispered, looking around the gloomy classroom as if expecting to see the monster already among them. "She shouldn't have sung it."

"Strikes me they were lucky," Daphne said. "I mean, Devin had to sing to call his wild beast. Ours is right here with us."

"Anne?" This from Shirley.

"No, silly," Daphne said, laughing. "I meant the Headmistress."

"I can't believe Anne was sent to the Red Room," Shirley said. "What did she do?"

"She was just being Anne," Mary replied. "Battling when surrender would better serve."

"I don't think so." Daphne leaned back in her chair and cupped her hands behind her head. "This time she may have blown her top for a reason. I think she saw Mary cover the bones, and I think she knew that if she didn't distract the Headmistress, we'd be sunk."

"You really think so?" Shirley asked.

"I do."

"So, she's like a hero?"

"Inasmuch as Anne can be heroic," Daphne

said. Deep down, she knew Anne was likely more worried about losing the bones herself. But regardless of motivation, she'd done a brave thing.

"I still find her crude," Mary said, lifting the Clutch. With long willowy fingers, she plucked the bones from her desk and dropped them into the bag one by one. "She's not nearly as congenial as Sylvia was." She lifted her head and fixed her eyes on the black glass of the broken window.

"The light of love, the purity of grace,
The mind, the music breathing from her
    face,
The heart whose softness harmonized
    the whole—
And, oh! that eye was in itself a Soul!"

"Is that another song?" Shirley asked.

"No, it's a poem," Mary replied. "Or at least, part of one. It's from Lord Byron. I thought about it earlier when we were talking about Sylvia, and it's just going round and round in my head."

"Well, I like that better than the monster song."

"I thought the song was rather pretty," Mary said.

"There was something haunting about it,"

Daphne agreed. "But speaking of monsters, we should check on Anne. Mary, you take the Clutch and hide the bones tonight. After what she's been through, I'm sure Anne won't want to be bothered with it."

"You won't say anything about the game?"

"No, Shirley. We won't say a word. Especially tonight. We should just be there for her and stay close."

Unbeknownst to the three, Anne was already close. She stood outside of the classroom, her back to the wall, her hearing tuned to the sound of their voices. She had arrived in time to see Mary gathering up the bones, just in time to hear her stupid poem.

They'd played without her, and they were going to pay for it.

"Speaking of monsters," Daphne had said, "we should check on Anne."

A monster, huh? She'd give them a monster, one they wouldn't soon forget.

TO BE CONTINUED

Don't Miss

WICKED DEAD

SNARED

She found the binoculars on the windowsill in the den. Lindsay certainly wasn't looking for them, but there they were. After dinner she'd wandered into the room, wanting to see more of the ocean. She picked the glasses up and lifted them to her eyes. The metal casing was heavy and cold against her soft skin. Looking through the lenses, she adjusted the focus until the distant ocean waves came to her crisp and clear, though still terribly gray from the storm. Breakers rose and crashed and foamed. It looked cool, if depressing. She swept the glasses over the horizon and down the beach, where she again adjusted the focus, bringing a new object into view.

"Jeez," Lindsay yelped, tearing the glasses from her eyes. There was something hideous and unbelievable out there. It looked like a baby, buried in the sand.

She looked through the binoculars again and relaxed. It was a doll. The plastic head was crushed and most of the body was buried in wet sand, but its sad and mangled face was clear enough. One of the eyes was open, while the other was covered with the broken eyelid, which drooped askance against the doll's cheek. The plastic fibers that once looked like hair fanned over the sand, dirty and wet.

Farther along, she saw the side of a distant house and then a window. Lindsay adjusted the focus yet again, and nearly dropped the binoculars when the image cleared.

A woman, maybe her mom's age but totally beautiful, walked through the upstairs bedroom of the house. She wore a brightly colored piece of fabric knotted around her waist. Its lovely purple and crimson swirls draped to the woman's knees. Besides the loose skirt, the woman was naked.

Embarrassed, Lindsay put the binoculars back on the sill and stepped away. It occurred to her that the half-naked woman was the exact reason her uncle Lou kept the binoculars on the sill, and she shuddered at the idea.

Still, she might be able to use the binoculars.

She wouldn't watch the boy next door, wouldn't spy on him or anything. But at least she could get a good look at him. More than likely he'd turn out to be just another guy, and that would be that. Though if he was cute . . .

The thing was, Lindsay had to take something good back from this trip, even if it was just a story about the hot guy next door. Her parents had dragged her away from the party of the year. That's all anyone would talk about when she got home, and Lindsay would feel like a complete shadow if she didn't have an equally cool—no, cooler—story to tell. She needed an adventure or a summer romance, something none of the other kids would have. She couldn't go home with stories about flea markets or rubbing suntan lotion on her mom's back.

Lindsay left the binoculars on the windowsill and walked through the dining room to the kitchen door. Wanting to make sure her parents were busy before she lifted the binoculars, Lindsay pushed open the swinging door and froze.

Her stomach knotted up, and she reared back a

step. Her parents were making out against the kitchen counter.

They weren't just kissing either. That was gross enough, but they were really lip-locked, and her mom had her hand inside her dad's shirt, rubbing his stomach. She didn't even want to think about where her dad's hands were.

At least they'd be busy for a while.

Lindsay closed the door quietly. She grabbed the binoculars and went up to her room.

Lindsay stood next to the window seat, adjusting the binoculars, focusing on the window of the house next door, but she didn't see the boy. The light was out in his room and not so much as a shadow moved. After a few minutes, she felt like a perv, and hid the binoculars under the green cushion before logging onto the web. She surfed around for a while, but the long day had exhausted her, and soon enough she turned off her computer and crossed the hall to the bathroom to brush her teeth.

Ten minutes later, she lay in bed and stared at the ceiling. The house was so quiet she could hear music playing next door. It was strange. It sounded New Agey, with the muffled chime of bells and a small drum being rapped beneath a moaning melody like chanting. Maybe the kid's grandparents were hippies or something. Her friend Trey's grandparents were like that. They wore headbands and said things like "groovy," "peace," and "far out" a lot. They really liked a place called Woodstock and a band called Happy Dead or something like that. Of course, Lindsay had no idea what that band sounded like. They might be just like the odd monotone voices she was hearing, punctuated by chimes and drums. They probably were.

Don't let it be his music, she thought. How sad would that be? A hot guy who listened to decaf tunes? That would be tear-worthy.

The moaning chant rose in volume, sounding deep and ominous.

Then a cry pierced through the muffled music. It sounded like someone was in pain. And it didn't seem to be part of the drum and chant song. Lindsay looked at the window, worried. Did someone outside need help?

Is it part of the song?

Afraid, Lindsay curled up tightly under the covers. The sound didn't come again, though she strained to hear. After a while, the music stopped and the night grew silent. Then she rolled over, faced the wall, and waited for sleep to come.

Lindsay woke to sunshine, the fear of the night forgotten. A wedge of golden light fell through the window, cutting a swath across the room and the end of her bed. Her parents moved around in their room at the other end of the hall. She heard their footsteps and their voices. Her mom giggled, and her dad made a growling noise. Lindsay did her best to ignore them. She felt great. Rested. Clearheaded. She wanted to pretend she was alone in this house and shared the beach with no one but the boy next door.

Lindsay rolled over and snuggled deeper into the quilt. He would be hot, she decided. No way did he listen to that hippie music. He would be young and cool and totally into extreme sports. A guy didn't get a body like that by playing video games all day. He was probably at the beach to surf. So cool. And he wouldn't be one of the immature guys she met at school. He'd be an adult, but not too old. *He'll be perfect,* she thought. *Just perfect.*

When she finally left her fantasy behind and got out of bed, she powered up her laptop and cast a glance out the window. No one moved in the yard or behind the windows of the rundown house. Disappointed, she grabbed her robe and put it on. Downstairs she found her parents in the kitchen again, only this time they weren't macking all over each other. That was a relief.

They exchanged good mornings and her dad, still smiling, asked if she'd slept well.

"Pretty good," she replied, heading directly for the coffeepot.

"It's the sea air."

"Mmmm," Lindsay replied, already deeply involved with her first cup of bean.

"I'm fixing pancakes," her mom said.

"Mom," Lindsay said, "you know I don't eat breakfast."

"You're on vacation."

"Try to convince my thighs," Lindsay said. "Thanks anyway. Coffee is fine."

She took her coffee upstairs and carried it to the window seat. After getting situated with her computer in her lap and her coffee next to her hip, she opened her email, but the house next door kept distracting her. She read a line of one of Trey's messages, looked down at the window, read another line. Kate sent an email telling her that Nick Faherty—only the hottest guy at school—was definitely going to be at her party and . . . *OMG, do you believe it? He's bringing his older brother who looks just like Tom Welling. I wish you could come. I'm going to be a total head case.*

Yes, you will, Lindsay thought. She looked through the window, thought she saw movement across the way, but the boy didn't appear.

Lindsay clicked the Reply button so she could tell Kate how happy she was for her. Nick and Ian Faherty were quite a party coup. It was epically unfair that Lindsay wouldn't be there to hang with them.

Before writing the note, she again looked out the window and was startled to see two men looking up at her from the backyard of the unpleasant house. The sight of them was unnerving. They just stood there, staring. But what really got to her was the fact that they were the same guys she'd seen at the grocery store wearing black parkas and holding huge umbrellas.

Today they wore black T-shirts and gray shorts. Both men seemed to be several years older than her dad but in infinitely better shape. The day before, she thought they were exact opposites, one skinny and one fat, but now she could see their muscle through their tight shirts. The short one was so buffed it looked like his shirt would tear open if he moved his arms at all. The tall one was narrower but ripped.

Lindsay looked away, hoping she hadn't stared too long. It was freaky enough to have them looking at her; she certainly didn't want to get caught staring back.

A thought began to emerge as she gazed at the blank email template on her screen. Maybe the boy next door had two fathers. He was the son of a gay couple. How cool would that be? Her friend Rachel had two moms, and they were really nice. Maybe the boy was adopted. That made him even more exotic. Another thought tried to creep in—a thought about the boy being something other than a son to these two men—but she pushed that away quickly. Life just couldn't be that unfair.

She threw another quick glance outside. The shorter man was pointing at the base of the house and talking to the taller man, who stooped to hear. The tall guy nodded his head. In the window, thirty feet from where these men examined the run-down house, the boy appeared.

Lindsay's heart raced, and she looked away to her computer screen. *Let him see you first*, she thought. *Don't let him catch you staring. He'll think you're a major freak. Just be cool. Pretend he isn't there and write back to Kate. Flip your hair just a bit, but don't look out the window. Smile like you've just thought of something brilliant. Drink some coffee. Hold the mug at your chin for a moment. Look up like your brilliant thought is totally deep. Put the mug down. Casually look out the window, and . . .*

The boy was gone. The two men in black T-shirts stared up at her from the backyard. Both looked pissed off.

Feeling uncomfortable under their gaze,

Lindsay lifted her laptop and carried it with her to the bed so she could write back to Kate.

Lindsay waited for her parents to leave for the flea markets before taking her shower and cleaning up for the day. She stood in front of the chest of drawers looking at the tops and the shorts she'd packed and didn't like any of them. All the clothes looked like something a little girl would wear, all pinks and yellows and whites. This always happened to her. Every time she *needed* to look good, she just couldn't find anything to wear. Most of her clothes were brand-new, but somewhere between the store rack and her uncle's house they'd lost their appeal. None of her outfits looked special enough. What if she ran into the boy outside? She didn't want to look like some Hicksville teen. Crap. These things were all she had, though. Something from the drawer would have to do. Finally she chose a pair of yellow shorts and took a white blouse from the closet.

Once dressed, she returned to the window for a moment to look down, but the boy wasn't there. She wandered downstairs and onto the porch of her uncle's house. The sky was clear and blue and the day hot, though the breeze off the ocean cooled her skin. Not far up the beach, she noticed the crowds. Dozens of people lay under the baking sun, walked over the sand, soaked in the ocean. She looked south and saw a handful of people there as well.

A car engine sputtered into life, and Lindsay backed toward the door. The noise came from behind the house next door, and she imagined the two old guys were going out for a drive. She walked into the house through the den and dining room to the kitchen door. She opened it, but did not step outside. Instead, she leaned on the jamb, making sure she was hidden from the driver's view.

She heard the car back out of the drive. Once she was certain it was far enough down the road, she poked her head out and saw the back of a long silver sedan. Sunlight glinted off its trunk as it rolled to the north. Satisfied that she could not be spotted, Lindsay walked onto the porch all the way to the rail.

On a whim, she walked to the side and looked over the rail down the length of the house to the window where she first saw the boy. From this angle, she couldn't see anything.

Lindsay walked back inside and up the stairs. In her room, she went immediately to the window seat and pressed her face against the glass, looking down at the boy's room.

And there he was.

He stood in the window. His head was lowered, looking at the band of sand separating his house from her uncle's. Lindsay pulled the binoculars from under the green cushion and quickly put them to her eyes. It took way too long for her to adjust the lenses, but finally the boy came into focus.

Excited, she waited for him to look up from the sandy ground. When he did, her throat closed up tight and her heart raced.

He *was* hot. As she expected, he was only a little older than her. Seventeen, maybe eighteen. His black hair jutted in wild spikes from his head. His thin face, flawless and beautiful, wore a sad expression that made Lindsay's heart flutter. His eyes were as blue as the sky. His frowning lips were full, and she suddenly wanted to kiss him, which was totally weird because she didn't even know him. But she found herself thrilled by the wonderment of what his lips might taste like and feel like against her own.

Lindsay spun from the window, clutching the binoculars to her chest. What was she going to do now? It wasn't like she could just go over to his house and say, "Hey, my parents dragged me out here from the city, and I got bored and was looking through my uncle's binoculars and thought you were hot, so why don't we date or something?"

She could sit in the window seat for a while and pretend to write on her laptop. He might see her, but then, he might not.

Her cell phone rang, yanking Lindsay from her thoughts. She checked the caller ID.

Kate.

"Perfect timing," Lindsay said as she answered the phone.

"What? What's going on?"

"Nine-one-one."

"More scary umbrella men?"

"Noooo," Lindsay said. "Jeez, live in the now. It's male-related."

"Beach hottie?"

"Way hottie. I mean, he's staying in the house

next door. I saw him through the window last night, and I thought he might be cute, but then I saw him again today, and he totally is. He's at his window right now."

"Is said hottie age-appropriate?" Kate asked.

"Duh."

"Any sign of female interference?"

"What? Like a girlfriend? I don't think so. The only other people I've seen at the house are a couple of old guys. I think they might be his parents."

"Both of them? Like Rachel's moms?"

"Pre-xactly like that. They're both buff, full-on groomed, and wear matching outfits."

"Sounds totally same-sex to me."

"I know," Lindsay said. "Progressive, right?"

"Do they really wear identical outfits? I mean, is it like they order from the same J.Crew catalogue or is it matching leather diapers or what?"

"Kate, come on."

"Okay," Kate said. "Is he still at the window?"

Lindsay leaned forward just enough to see the boy in the neighboring house. "Yes."

"Well, what are you going to do?"

She thought about it for a moment and came up with a plan. It was simple and cool. It made her smile. "We're going for a walk," Lindsay said.

"I can't," Lindsay said, standing on the sand behind her uncle's house.

"Well, I know I couldn't, but you can," Kate said. "You can do anything. Besides, it's no crisis. You're just talking on the phone, wandering around the yard. No big deal. You don't even know he exists. It's a total coincidence. Now, set to steppin'. I have a bazillion things to do before the party."

"I'm so pissed I can't be there."

"I know," Kate said. "It's totally lame. There's no way I can pull this off without you here. I mean, what if we run out of beer or something? Or what if Matt starts a fight? Crap. I should just cancel."

"You can't cancel. If you're worried about the beer, just have Matt's brother pick up a couple of extra cases. Put them in the bathroom off the kitchen, in the tub, and cover them with ice. As for Matt, he isn't going to start a fight, because his mother threatened to yank him off the basketball team if he caused any more trouble. If he gets all weird, just remind him of that."

"I will," Kate said. "You're right. Thanks."

"No problem."

"I promise I'll take a ton of pictures and post them on my website. It'll be kind of like being there."

"Uh-huh." And watching the Oscars on television was kind of like being Colin Farrell's date. "Now, I'm about to make contact."

Lindsay shook out her free hand to relieve a bit of stress. She rolled her head on her neck and then stepped onto the band of sand between the two houses. Though she tried to resist, she threw a quick glance at the boy's window. Catching herself, she looked away quickly before she could even tell if he was there. Instead she looked down and noticed for the first time that her uncle's house didn't rest on the ground. It stood three feet above the sand on wooden supports. In the shadows under the house, tufts of tall grasses grew.

"That's weird," she said.

"What? Is he gross close-up?"

"No," Lindsay said. "We've come to my uncle's a bunch of times before, and I never noticed that his house is built up off the ground."

"Yeah, fascinating," Kate said, her voice thick with sarcasm. "Architecture is hot. What's *the boy* doing?"

"I haven't looked over there yet. Should I?"

"Yeah, but let me say something funny first. That way, he'll see you smiling."

"Okay."

"On the count of three," Kate said. "Ready? One, two . . ."

Lindsay began to turn, hoping the boy would still be in his window when she completed the turn.